HOW TO GET AWAY WITH *EVIL*

ENYA CLANCY

To everyone

who read the first (horrible) draft of the novel

and didn't laugh when fourteen-year-old me said,

"Someday, I'm going to get this published."

Playlist

"Mr. Sandman" ~ The Chordettes

"Sweet Little Lies" ~ büllow

"Killer" ~ CHVRCHES

"I Knew You Were Trouble" ~ Taylor Swift

"All Comes Crashing" ~ Metric

"brutal" ~ Olivia Rodrigo

"High" ~ Sir Sly

"Darkest Hour" ~ Tate McRae

"In My Head" ~ Kailee Morgue & Mike Shinoda

"Karma" ~ Taylor Swift

"I'm Full" ~ Wallows

"Wolf" ~ Yeah Yeah Yeahs

"Trouble" ~ Cage The Elephant

"Heaven Knows" ~ The Pretty Reckless

"Born to Die" ~ Lana Del Rey

It all begins and ends in your mind.

What you give power to, has power over you,

if you allow it.

–Unknown

August 2nd, 2015 – 12:01 AM

W hat's going on?" I shrieked, staring at the person that I could no longer recognize. The figure, who was lurking in the shadows of the kitchen, looked exactly like all the killers I had seen in horror movies – dark, tall, and ready to slash the life out of their victims.

It didn't make sense.

I was no saint, but I couldn't remember doing anything to them to deserve this.

That didn't stop them, though, from charging toward me in the creepy room, rattling the spoons that hung above the sink. I backed up quickly into the corner of the counter, my hand fumbling behind me as I tried to find something sharp to defend myself with.

Before I could scream, their hand clamped over my mouth. The figure then pulled one of the sharpest knives out of the knife block on the counter behind me. The weapon glimmered eerily in the light of the full moon that poured in through the kitchen window.

I tried to bite one of the killer's fingers that covered my mouth, hoping that it would startle them away from me. But the leather gloves that they were now wearing were surely too thick for them to have felt anything.

I tried to pull away, but the hem of my silky, lilac nightgown snagged on the dishtowel hook under the sink, capturing me in place.

I'm dead.

A collage of memories started to flood my mind, my entire life flashing before my eyes. My heart raced in my chest, and my body trembled as the inevitable sank in.

My life's over. My life's actually *over–*

I coughed as I felt the oxygen from my lungs get ripped out of me. I looked down and noticed that the knife was deeply plunged into the side of my neck.

Black spots blurred my vision.

I began to sway.

I can't die, I can't die, I can't–

Chapter 1
Adley
The Guilty Girl's Handbook

The last thing I would have expected on August second was to be awoken by a scream.

Jessi and I shot up, frightened and confused, each then glancing at the other from our sleeping bags. Instantly, we threw ourselves out of the bedroom and down the creaky steps of the steep staircase, Jessi tripping and nearly falling down the stairs.

As the two of us filed into the dining room where Mr. and Mrs. Landers stood, blocking the entrance to the kitchen, I crashed into Ethan, who was in tears. He kept wiping them away with a shaking hand, and I questioned for a second what could possibly be going on–

A flash of blood obscured my vision, a memory of leather gloves and a blood-splattered, glimmering knife flashing before my eyes.

No, it couldn't *have happened.*

Confusion clouding my mind, I advanced toward

everyone, alongside Jessi. I then covered my mouth with a hand in shock when I saw the truth.

There, lying motionless on the gray kitchen tiles, the right side of her throat and body caked in dried blood, was my best friend. Her spaghetti-strapped lilac nightgown was torn at the white-laced hem, a piece of material hooked onto the silver dish towel hanger.

No.

"Wh-What happened?" stammered Jessi, her brown eyes wide, and her face drained of color.

No, I kept repeating, my heartbeat quickening. *This can't be happening.*

"We think someone came after her last night," Ethan explained his voice shaking as he stared at the scene in front of us.

I couldn't remove my eyes from the limp body either, so in shock that I couldn't process anything. All I could think was that I was in a dream, and that any second, I would wake up and everything would be okay.

"This *can't* be happening." Tears spilled down Jessi's cheeks, and she shook her head, her hand covering her mouth. "Tell me that Annabeth isn't–?"

"Dead." Ethan and Jessi snapped their heads around to look at me, though I kept my focus on the floor. "She's gone, isn't she?"

Jessi suddenly burst into tears, shaking uncontrollably. I couldn't believe it – my best friend was gone, and there was nothing that I was able to do to change that.

Ethan nodded in reply to my question, then took a

step closer to Jessi and wrapped an arm around her shoulders, trying to make her feel better. It didn't look as if he was helping. "My parents said it had to be a murder. It doesn't make sense as to why this would have happened. They found one of the kitchen knives covered in blood next to Anna, and they also came upon this."

Leaving Jessi's side next to the oak dining room table, he motioned for us to follow him. Jessi and I walked past his parents, who were each talking low on their phones, and entered deeper into the kitchen. On the kitchen island, Anna's brand-new iPhone sat in the peach-pink case she'd gotten for her birthday. After Ethan unlocked the phone, I saw that *911* had been typed into the phone keypad.

I then glanced to the floor, where I spotted the sharp knife, droplets of ruby-red blood decorating its surface. I looked from the knife to Anna's neck.

Of course, a deep stab into the side of the neck. No wonder it's a famous move for killers in horror movies – the victims barely ever live through it.

The thought ran a shiver down my spine.

"I'm so sorry," started Mrs. Landers, startling me as she joined us. She had stopped crying, but her hands were cold and wet from wiping away tears when she placed them on my bare shoulders. "This-this must be very hard for you to see…"

"The cops will be here any minute," Mr. Landers added monotonously, joining us near the counter. He was never good at dealing with emotional situations. "Why don't you head upstairs and get ready?" Once we all nodded, he added, looking toward me and Jessi, "And call your parents.

I'm sure they'll want to know what… what has happened."

"Of course," I responded quietly. I then passed Ethan and quickly made my way up the stairs to the second floor, Jessi following behind me.

It was as I reached the top of the steps that a feeling of emptiness filled me. But once I counted all ten of my fingers, I knew that this couldn't be just a dream.

"I don't get it. Who would have ever wanted Annabeth Landers *dead*?" Jessi questioned after she had changed out of her plaid pajamas and into a pair of blue jeans and a black t-shirt. She paced back and forth across Anna's bedroom, chewing her already damaged nails nervously as curiosity took over her pain. "She-she was so sweet and kind…"

"Um, remember how she *stole* my sweater last week–?"

"Adley!" Jessi scolded, turning to face me with a scowl before going back to pacing. "Is that seriously the only thing that comes to mind when you think about our *best friend*?"

I tried my hardest not to roll my eyes when she called Anna *our* best friend – now wasn't the time. "I was just *reminiscing*," I defended, laughing shakily in an attempt to lighten the mood as I tossed my toiletries into my overnight bag.

Jessi stopped pacing, staring blankly at one of Anna's cotton candy-pink walls – the room now felt oddly empty and lifeless without her.

When Jessi didn't look away after a few moments, her eyes now glued to the large window, I asked, "Hey, Jess?

Are you okay?"

"Yeah," she responded, then shook her head, sending messy strands of her copper-streaked, deep-brown hair flying. "I mean, no. I mean…"

"It was a stupid question," I admitted, looking down at my toes, their ruby-red nail polish sending shivers up my spine. It was too similar to the blood that I kept seeing everywhere I turned.

"It's just… How can *anyone* be okay, knowing that someone so… so *perfect* can just *die*? That everything someone could be going for could end so easily? There-there's just so much that Anna never got to *do*–" Jessi cut herself off, and I noticed as I followed her gaze out the bedroom window that the cops had arrived. Red and blue lights bounced off the houses in the neighborhood, and loud voices abruptly boomed from downstairs, slicing through the silence.

Curious to know what was going on, the two of us exited the bedroom and ran to the hallway banister, hoping to get a glimpse of what was going on downstairs. We were out of luck, though, so I turned away and headed back into Anna's room to change.

As I got dressed, slipping on a pair of high-waisted denim shorts, I heard a string of text messages come in from my phone.

Mom
7:55 AM
What's with the police over at Annabeth's house?
Are you okay?

You better not be ignoring me.

I had completely forgotten about messaging her.

I lived in the house across from Anna's, so my mom always knew what was going on. Especially when Anna and Ethan would get into a fight over something as stupid as a missing Barbie doll.

That was how I had met Anna, actually. I had been the first to become close friends with her by finding her Barbie doll on the sidewalk. It had been right before she and Ethan, her twin brother, had gotten into a tug-a-war fight with a piece of chalk during the summer when we were five years old. They had just moved to the neighborhood, and after I had returned the doll and had helped them solve their problem by breaking the stick of pink chalk in half, they had invited me to play with them.

It hadn't taken long before Anna and I were attached by the hip, doing *everything* together.

As I stood in her bedroom, remembering these times and chuckling softly to myself, my heart squeezed.

This is all your fault, the little voice in the back of my head kept chanting, but I pushed it aside. *It can't be,* I assured myself. *All I remember are similar fragments... moments of a dream – not my friend's death. It's all just a coincidence.*

After replying to my mom, explaining that I would be home soon, I threw on my turquoise shirt and joined Jessi as she marched back downstairs with her beaten, pink Roots backpack slung over her shoulder.

"We were just about to come to see you," Mr. Landers remarked from the bottom of the stairs, making me and Jessi halt. "We wanted to inform you that the knife was tested for finger prints but only showed ours since it was our knife."

"That's why we'd like to test everyone from the crime scene to see if we need to pull you in for questioning," a tall man in a navy-blue "Ember Falls, Wisconsin" police uniform informed.

"*Questioning*?" My eyes widened in alarm, and I felt beads of sweat form on my forehead.

Shit, they actually think that the killer is one of us.

And what if it is?

After clearing the small glass table and tan-colored sofa, which had been covered with DVDs and Wii remotes from the night before, Ethan, Jessi, and I were instructed to prick our index fingers on a needle-looking device.

How things worked in our town when it came to see who was guilty was drawing blood. It was my first time having the Test done, but scientists had claimed a few years back that if your blood appeared any shade between gray and black when smeared on the white Tester paper, it showed that you were guilty of *something* – possibly the crime that you were being Tested for. The blacker your blood was, the guiltier you supposedly were. It was better and way more accurate, they said, compared to any lie detector test.

That scared the shit out of me.

Ethan went first, wincing at the prick as he looked into my eyes. His blood was mostly red but had swirls of steel gray in it. Therefore, he was still considered a suspect, as stupid as that was.

Then, Jessi went, who we all knew was guilty of nothing. As much of an angel as Annabeth was known as, Jessi was the real saint who *never* did anything wrong.

However, her blood was *dark gray.*

And if her blood is that dark, mine will be as black as midnight.

As the police officer's intense eyes punctured my thoughts, forcing me to sit down, my heartbeat sped up.

I've got to act natural. They can't suspect anything.

So, I pierced my finger, and with a burning pinch, blood was drawn, which I shakily wiped onto a strip of Tester paper. I closed my eyes for a second, preparing for the inevitable. When I heard no comments about my results, I opened my eyes.

What?

It made no sense.

I blinked, then looked back at the Tester paper. My blood was revealed to be pure, ruby red with not a single touch of guilt.

"Hey, look how lucky you are," laughed Jessi, an unusual giddiness consuming her, probably due to the nerves she now had. She pointed to the Tester paper. "How can you be innocent when I'm not? Wow, the times have changed."

"Yeah," I agreed, still not believing the sight.

"Sorry to cut this conversation of yours short, but we better bring you in for questioning before rush hour starts. Do you mind getting on with me and having a guardian meet us at the station?" the police officer asked, looking at Jessi and Ethan.

Nodding, the two of them slowly made their way to the front entrance and put on their shoes. I trailed behind them, leaning against the doorway and fighting the tears that were threatening to spill from my eyes.

Ethan turned around, shooting me a sad smile. "Well, um, bye, Adley."

I approached him cautiously, afraid that the police officers might yell at me. Then, without thinking, I threw my arms around his neck and hugged him hard. "I am so, *so* sorry about Anna," I whispered.

Ethan sniffled, wiping away a tear, as we broke apart. "I know you are. You were a sister to her."

I felt my lip tremble. I knew that I was dangerously close to crying, but I forced myself to stay composed.

As soon as Jessi and Ethan, followed by Mr. Landers and the police, stepped outside, the door clicked shut behind them, and I broke apart. I fell to the floor, cupping my hands over my face and sobbing.

Another flash of blood obscured my vision. This time, though, I then saw Anna's petrified face right before a knife was plunged into the side of her neck.

"Adley, sweetheart," Mrs. Landers cooed, kneeling beside me and gently touching my shoulder. "This is not your fault."

But it is.

I stayed silent, trying desperately to compose myself. There had to have been a problem with the Tester because I knew that I was guilty – these visions proved it. Besides, I was that crazy teenager in our gang who'd do things that nobody else would – why wasn't *I* claimed guilty?

It made no sense.

I had gotten drunk multiple times before. I had stolen sunglasses from Sunglass Hut just a week ago. I had broken curfew five times in the past month. I had done so many things that I would take with me to my grave.

And in this case, also Anna's grave.

Because even though I couldn't remember why or what had exactly led me to do so, I knew that I had been the last one to see Annabeth before she died.

I had been the one to kill her.

And with this investigation beginning, someone else was bound to find out eventually.

Chapter 2
Jessi
Jail isn't for Angels

Annabeth was dead, and it hadn't been an accident.

That was all I knew.

I didn't understand *how* or *why* someone would *kill* Anna. She had been the closest to perfect that I had ever known. She was the type of person who made you feel lucky just for knowing them – the type of person who never faltered or doubted themselves.

Basically, everything that *I* wasn't.

I stared out of the barred window of the police car, trying to ignore how ridiculously tight the backseat was, only made worse by the fact that Ethan was squeezed in beside me. I wanted to scream, to claw and pound at the windows until they let me out so that I could run far, *far* away–

No, I told myself. *Stay calm. Acting like a psychopath won't help you.*

The scratchy, frayed seatbelt rubbed uncomfortably against my neck, and I tried to sit up straighter, but that didn't fix the problem. I had always been the shortest, and the world seemed to love reminding me of that.

Continuing to stare out the window, I suddenly caught a glimpse of my disastrous reflection – messy hair; eyes rimmed with shadows; obnoxiously obvious reddish-brown birthmark that circled my right eye like a bruise.

I quickly averted my eyes from my reflection and glanced over at Ethan, who was staring blankly ahead, anxiously twisting his fingers in his lap.

I can't believe they even consider him a suspect, I thought, chewing one of my nails.

Ethan looked over at me, then shot me a concerned, disapproving glance. I stopped biting. Brushing a lock of chin-length hair out of my face, I leaned against the car door, trying to keep my breathing even.

Suddenly, the police car jolted to a stop, hurling me forward in my seat.

We were there.

At the *police station*.

I swallowed hard, my heart pounding. I had promised my dad that I would *never* end up here, yet here I was.

One of the police officers, who I had nicknamed Blondie due to his blond curls, opened my door. And – since I had been leaning against the door – I was sent toppling onto the uneven sidewalk. I would have face-planted into the cement had it not been for my *excellent* reflexes.

I looked back at Blondie, but he was too busy trying to get Ethan – who seemed to be frozen in fear – out of the car. I huffed and pulled myself off the pavement, more annoyed than hurt.

"Single-file, please," ordered another cop – his name tag reading "Officer Hale."

His perfect posture and loud voice made me reluctant to follow his commands. I took my spot in front of Ethan, and Blondie walked beside me as if I might lash out at any moment and would need him to restrain me. I felt then a familiar, uneasy, tight feeling in my chest, which only reminded me of how I always felt around Adley.

She and I had never been *super*-close friends, but whenever I was with her, I would feel this tugging in my chest – a physical repulsion, like two magnets with their poles facing each other.

It always made me feel like I should run, but I didn't know why.

As Blondie shoved open the door to the police station, the smell of antiseptic immediately smacked me in the face. I flinched, scrunching up my nose. The officer seemed to notice my reaction and glared a warning my way.

I couldn't believe them, hardly giving me a break when my best friend had just *died*. Hell, I was trying my best not to cry since I knew that once I'd start, I'd never finish.

I looked away from Blondie's stare and around the lobby. In sum, with its dimly lit lights, it looked like a creepy hospital from a thriller that I had once watched with Anna. There were two rows of dark blue hard-plastic chairs – the kind that left marks on your thighs – and a reception desk, where an exhausted-looking police officer sat, rifling through some paperwork.

She looked up when Blondie cleared his throat, her

dull, green eyes squinting at us. "Officer Porter," she said to Blondie with a thick southern accent, then glanced over at me, her gaze lingering on my birthmark. "What can I do for y'all?"

"Are any of the rooms free?" Blondie – or Officer Porter, as I probably should have been calling him – asked, though the station was deserted.

"Room five is available," the tired police officer responded, tucking a strand of black hair behind her ear. "So are rooms six, twelve, and thirteen–"

"Thank you, Officer Johnson," Officer Porter said before directing me and Ethan to the rows of chairs, where he made us sit down.

I was about to sit next to Ethan until Officer Porter took that spot and made me sit beside *him,* Officer Hale sitting on my other side.

Jeez, I thought to myself. *Are they that afraid that I'm going to do something?*

My blood had come back darker than everyone else's – by a lot – but that didn't mean that I was a grade-A maniac.

At least, I didn't *feel* like one.

Unless that's what all maniacs say...

In any case, I hadn't committed any murders.

Especially not Anna's.

Officer Porter's beady blue eyes, suddenly boring into my own, shook me from my thoughts. I sat up straighter, the rigid plastic of the chair knocking against my spine.

"Is there a parent or legal guardian that you would be able to reach?" he asked me, looking like Adley during math class – bored and waiting for the hour of pointlessness to be over.

A sharp panic seized me. I only had my dad whom I could call, and *God*, I did *not* want to. Having a lawyer as a parent during a police interrogation could be helpful, but I could already picture the *many* ways it could go downhill.

"Father?" Officer Hale prompted, hoping that I'd talk. "Mother?"

Well, I didn't have much luck in that department since the only mother that I had was long gone in bright, sunny *California.* She had dumped me – a month-old baby – in my dad's arms, had left, and had never looked back.

"I can call my dad," I said slowly, knowing that there was no other answer.

Officer Porter nodded sharply. "Good. Do you have access to a phone?"

"Yeah," I answered, fishing my BlackBerry out of my embarrassingly messy backpack.

"Perfect," Officer Porter responded, then wandered over to talk to Mr. Landers, who had just arrived through the police department's front doors.

I dialed my dad's number excruciatingly slowly, and when he picked up, my heartbeat sped up. "Hey, Dad?" I took a deep breath, then stated, "I'm at the police station."

Half an hour later, seated tensely beside my dad in room thirteen – *bad luck right off the bat* – I watched intently as a police officer scribbled down what little information I had so far given her about myself.

The police officer – whose badge read "Officer

Roden" – looked up from her clipboard and straight at me, her face stern. "Jessi Cecilia" –I found myself flinching at the name, then tried hard to forget the image of my mother that popped into my mind– "Alvarez. Before we get into this, we'd like to remind you that we have no intention of being harsh. We would just like to know the truth. For starters, why don't you explain why you were at the Landers' house this morning?"

"I–" my voice trembled, so I cleared my throat. "I was there since Annabeth had invited me and Adley over for a sleepover. We did these all the time – board games, Just Dance, movie marathons–" I cut myself off and blushed when I realized that I was rambling, then started chewing a nail to shut myself up.

Officer Roden nodded as she scribbled a few notes down. "Okay. Next, could you tell me about your ties to Miss Landers?"

"I met Ann–" I stopped halfway through Anna's name – just saying it felt too painful, and it only brought back images of her lying dead, cold, and bloody on her kitchen floor. I bit my lip, shaking myself from my thoughts. "I met her at volleyball camp when we were fourteen. We then started at Ember Falls High together that year, and we played on the same volleyball team. She annoyed the crap out of me with all her perfect serves." I laughed softly, though I knew it was a super inappropriate time. "I'm sorry, I'm rambling again."

"That's perfectly all right, Miss Alvarez," said Officer Roden. "It seems that you and Miss Landers were close. However, that brings us to the subject of your Test."

I swallowed hard, feeling my pulse speed up.

"As you probably know," Officer Roden stated, "your blood came back very dark. Do you think you can explain why?"

I tried desperately to hide my panic, smoothing out my features and giving an innocent shrug. I had no clue how to answer.

"Please, Miss Alvarez," Officer Roden sighed, rubbing her eyes. "This will go over much easier if you cooperate."

"I didn't do anything!" I shouted, my voice sounding desperate. "I would never, *ever,* in my life, hurt Annabeth."

"Perhaps not, Miss Alvarez, but the Test does not lie. You've obviously done something significant for your blood to be that dark."

"I haven't done *anything*," I said, my voice turning soft and meek. "Ask anyone."

"Miss Alvarez, please. Collaboration is key during moments like these. We need all the information we can get."

"I don't know anything," I repeated, fighting the urge to break down into tears. "Please, I just want to go home." I bit my lip until I tasted blood, fighting the urge to get up and run out of the room.

Officer Roden sighed, exasperated by my stubbornness. "Miss Alvarez–"

"That's *enough,*" my dad said suddenly, standing up and putting a hand on my shoulder. "My daughter has nothing more to add." He shook his head slowly. "You cannot seriously believe that she or Ethan Landers are responsible."

"Every person is a valuable asset," Officer Roden stated calmly, combing a hand through her dark, frizzy hair.

My dad shook his head again but didn't add anything else.

Officer Roden sighed, rubbing her temples with her fingertips as if we had given her a headache. "Very well, then. You are free to go, Miss Alvarez."

I leaped up from my seat, almost sending my chair toppling onto the ground.

Just as I turned to leave, though, Officer Roden spoke. "You may not have anything more to add at the moment, Miss Alvarez. But should we discover that you are hiding vital information from us, you may find yourself in this room once again."

My dad looked at Officer Roden, his face unreadable. Then, he nudged me out of the room without giving me the chance to say anything back.

I hadn't stopped thinking about the investigation the entire day. After all, the doors had been locked, and there had been no broken windows. something *else* had to have happened the night that Anna was murdered.

I had convinced Ethan, along with everyone else, after the interrogation that I was going to let the cops handle everything now. At least, that *was* until I had crafted a magnificent plan that Adley was going to help me with.

I stepped into Danny's Diner, the popular hangout spot in Ember Falls where I had messaged Adley to meet me at. I wrung out my drenched hair as a gust of chilly air from the air conditioning smacked me in the face. I shivered, cursing myself for having forgotten my raincoat. The rain had never been a particular pet peeve of mine – I would even go as far as to say that I actually *enjoyed* it – but, at the moment, I was not exactly appreciating it.

Shivering, I headed over to the diner's counter, where I ordered myself my usual drink: the tiniest amount of coffee, loads of sugar, a healthy dose of cream, and, of course, a generous sprinkling of cinnamon. I then tried to gracefully slide onto one of the bright red high stools, but that was impossible with my lack of height. I ended up struggling, gripping the counter, and pulling myself up, as usual.

"Having trouble, Short Stack?"

I flinched at the teasing voice, knowing *exactly* who was behind me. I rolled my eyes.

Ivy Blackthorn strode over to the counter and swung her long legs over the stool gracefully as if to rub in the fact that I would never be as tall and cool as she was. She flipped a lock of damp, green-streaked, black hair over her shoulder, smirking at me in that irritating way of hers. "Still mastering the art of living in a full-size world?" she asked after ordering herself a caramel macchiato.

"Very funny," I grumbled, though I was shocked, if not also angry, to see her back in town.

Ivy had suddenly left a year ago – to visit family in Paris, *apparently* – and I couldn't say that I had minded having her gone. Ivy and I weren't friends, and damn, did she *ever* get on my nerves. She also made me a little nervous with her black leather jacket, spiky-toed combat boots, and overall *height* – she was taller than... pretty much *everyone.*

"Where's your little girlfriend?" Ivy asked, and I immediately knew that she was referring to Annabeth. The two of us had been close, but I *seriously* didn't understand where Ivy had gotten *that* idea. With the number of boys that Anna had dated...

I would never have had a chance.

I glared back at Ivy, feeling my fists clench as we were given our drinks. I took a sip of mine, trying to calm myself down, but it didn't help.

Where is Annabeth? I wanted to scream. *Oh, I know* exactly *where she is.*

"She's *dead!*" I shouted at Ivy, then smacked my hands over my mouth. Thankfully, the diner was deserted at that hour, and even the waiters were in the back, probably now lounging in the kitchen.

Ivy's cool composure broke, and shock flashed across her face before she stuck her usual I-Don't-Care-About-Anything look back on. "You better not be fishing for sympathy after your big break-up, Short Stack. Breaking up doesn't mean that she's dead–"

"Shut up!" I snarled as I felt heat rush to my cheeks despite the inappropriate situation. "We were never a thing! We didn't *break up*! She's *dead*! *Morte! Muerta!* Need it in another language, or is it *finally* getting past that thick skull of yours?"

Ivy's face twisted with an emotion I couldn't quite describe – maybe something between insulted and shocked. "Wow. Okay, then," she said with so little emotion that I wanted to punch her. "Well, sorry for your loss." She then stood up and snatched her drink from the counter before heading out of the diner.

I took another sip of my coffee, trying to cool off, then nearly choked, as I heard the jingling of the little bell above the diner door. I spun around on my stool so quickly that I nearly fell off, then caught sight of Adley. She was wearing her raincoat and carrying a black umbrella as if she, of all people, had been thoroughly prepared for the rainstorm. I hopped off the stool, carrying my precious mug of coffee, and made my way over to Adley.

However, as I got closer to her, I noticed that she looked like she'd just crawled out of the sixth circle of Hell. Her dark blonde hair was a mess of tangles, her brown eyes were rimmed with shadows, and her walk had lost its usual confident quality. Her shoulders were curled in ever so slightly, and she was shuffling, scuffing the toes of her laced-up platform boots on the tiles of the floor. Adley had always been a fashionista, constantly trying to get me to wear something other than overalls and baggy t-shirts – something to "flatter my figure" – so seeing her treat her high-quality boots like that was a clear sign that she was not doing well.

"Hey," I said, keeping my hands cupped around my warm mug.

"Oh, hey," Adley mumbled, then wandered over to our usual booth at the back of the diner. She slid into the booth, her bloodshot eyes staring blankly ahead.

I sat in front of her, ignoring the strange feeling in my chest, and pushed my mug toward her. She looked at the steaming, pale brown liquid in the cup, then up at me, eyes questioning. "Have some," I offered. Adley started to refuse, but I pushed the mug closer to her. "I *insist*. It'll help."

Adley smiled sadly at me. "Thanks," she whispered before taking a sip. Then, she smirked ever so slightly. "*Please,* don't tell me that you *actually* consider this coffee, Jessi. This is cinnamon and cream."

I reached across the table and punched her arm teasingly. "Not everyone can drink black coffee, Adley."

"God, what I drink is *far* from black coffee, but it's *actually* coffee."

I stuck my tongue out at her, nearly recoiling as the feeling in my chest pushed back so hard that it hurt. I still didn't know why I felt like that around her, but I had concluded that I was just nervous around her because of who she *was.*

After all, she had a rebellious character that I could never even get close to matching, and the fact that her school track and field jersey number was thirteen didn't sit well with me.

"So, what exactly are we doing here, Jess?" Adley asked, rubbing her eyes and smudging her mascara. She didn't seem to care, though.

"We," I began slowly, with a small smile, "are going to figure out who killed our best friend."

Chapter 3
Adley
Blood is the New Black

Adley? Earth to Adley!" A blurry hand swiftly waved in front of my tired eyes, and once I noticed it was Jessi's voice that I was hearing, everything came back into focus.

"*W-What* is it?" I looked around alarmingly and noticed that I was seated in one of the dull, blue leather-seated booths in Danny's Diner. Jessi was staring at me from across the table as if I had three heads. A little creeped out and not thinking twice, I grabbed the cream-colored coffee mug in front of me. I then took a sip of this insanely-sweet beverage that reminded me of a hot, melted cinnamon milkshake. My lips puckered, disgusted. "Jessi, how many times am I gonna have to say this? This isn't–"

"*Coffee,* I know. You just told me." Tugging the mug out of my hands, Jessi sighed and took a sip of her drink. "Adley, what's up? You haven't been like this since sophomore year when that *jerk* broke your heart."

I felt a tightness in my chest for a second, the thought

of my ex-boyfriend – who Jessi didn't particularly *like* – making me wince. I didn't comment, tearing a hand through my blonde, tangled knots and staring down at the table.

Nate Tucker had been my first boyfriend after weeks of flirting in the halls during our first year of high school. However, he had broken up with me at the start of our sophomore year since he was leaving for New York City. I would have been lying if I said that I was over him – because I *wasn't* – but I knew that I was never going to see him again, and hoping was only going to lead to more heartbreak.

"Today has just been a really hard day," I explained, replying to Jessi's question but ignoring the mention of Nate. "I think we can both agree on that. So, to get back on track, we are here to…?"

"Discuss how we're going to find Anna's killer," Jessi answered, confused by how I had already forgotten.

Oh, yeah.

To be perfectly honest, I had never *agreed* to this plan. Jessi had just texted me as vaguely as possible, asking me if I would be up to playing some game, before telling me to meet her at the diner. It was only after sitting in our usual booth that she dropped the whole We-Are-Looking-For-Anna's-Killer bombshell.

Of course, I couldn't just say no since I would have looked suspicious. I had to help Jessi find out who killed our best friend, even if I knew that it had been *me*. Playing along would keep me off her radar, after all. My only issue now was creating a plan to make sure that I wouldn't get caught in the end – which wasn't as simple as I thought it would be.

"I was thinking that we just ask her–"

"*Ask* her?" I whisper-cried, cutting Jessi off as my heartbeat sped up. "Jess, she's gone. So unless you can magically talk to the dead, your plan isn't going to work."

Jessi pressed a hand to her chest as if she was feeling physical pain from my comment. "It's called using a Ouija board," Jessi declared matter-of-factly. "If we can interact with Anna that way, *maybe* she can tell us who murdered her."

"Do you actually think she *knows* who killed her?" I asked, fear creeping into my thoughts.

If we talk to Anna, I'll be caught right away. She knows I killed her, and she'll rat me out in seconds.

"Honestly, it's a fifty-fifty chance, but it's worth a shot." Jessi's already-wide eyes got bigger, as she stared at my hands intensely. I followed her gaze to notice that my hands were shaking, and I quickly tucked them into the sleeves of my black rain jacket. "Adley, you're freezing!" she cried, and I rolled my eyes.

Jessi and I had a *very* interesting dynamic. Anna and I had become friends when we were little, but when Anna had left for volleyball camp the summer before high school, she had met Jessi. From the start, Jessi and I never got along, but Anna loved having Jessi around. So, since then, we had been a trio who had done *everything* together, no matter if I truly liked Jessi or not. My feelings toward Jessi were probably obvious, yet she still tried to act like we were *best friends.* But, with Anna gone now, I had no clue where we stood.

"I'm fine—"

"I'm going to go order you a drink," Jessi told me, as

she stood up from her seat. "I'll be right back." Before I could stop her, Jessi was making her way toward the counter across the diner, and I slouched even more in my spot.

"No one can find out," I heard a small but powerful voice suddenly say, making me turn to look behind. There sat an empty booth with nothing but an *Ember Falls Weekly* newspaper sitting on the coffee-stained table.

Perplexed, I began to examine the diner, though the room was deserted with only one other booth occupied. Nothing looked out of the ordinary – at least, not for an 80s-inspired diner, with vibrant green and blue walls, black-and-white checkered flooring tiles, and metal high-tables and stools that dotted around the spacious area. The diner was quiet besides the faint music coming from the jukebox in the corner adjacent to me, "Mr. Sandman" by The Chordettes whisking me away from my worries for a moment.

"You must change her mind," I heard the same voice say, this time sounding more desperate. I picked up that it was a man's, which was weird since there were no guys around.

I was freakishly confused until I noticed this familiarity in the voice. It wasn't someone I particularly knew, but it matched the strange, repetitive voice in my head that would whisper to me the crazy ideas that I would always have.

The little devil that sat on my shoulder.

Oh, shit! I am *going insane,* I thought before trying to roll off the idea. *I'm not going insane, I'm not going insane, I'm not–*

"So," Jessi remarked, dragging out the single word,

as she sat back down and slid a mug of hot chocolate my way. "Are you going to help me?"

"Talk to Anna?" I clarified, shaking out of my daze, and trying not to sound terrified by the idea. "Um, yeah... Sure, I'm in."

Passing by the Landers' house on my way home from the diner gave me shivers and knots in my stomach. I tried to sprint by quickly before anyone could stop me and ask how I was doing because I couldn't stand the sympathy anymore.

I didn't *deserve* it.

All my plans came crashing down as I saw Ethan, though, his golden curls blowing in the cool early evening breeze. He was sitting on the wooden steps of his tall, blue Victorian house, and I noticed that he was alone – the car wasn't in the driveway, meaning that his parents had left. Ethan was looking down and fidgeting with a once-folded piece of paper, while his lips moved but no words came out of his mouth.

I hated what I had done to him, and I couldn't just ignore him now.

"Where are your parents?" I called to him from the sidewalk.

Ethan looked up from the paper as his brown eyes grew wide. "At the police station answering questions."

"Their blood was dark?" I asked, shocked by the thought. His parents were angels – always letting me sleep at their house when times would get rough at home; always letting me talk out my problems with them; always making those Ants-On-A-Log as an afternoon snack whenever I came over to do homework.

I had always wished that I had been born into their family.

Sometimes I hated mine.

"Nah, it was a protocol that the police had to do. Just basic family questioning," Ethan explained. "They should be back soon."

"How was the interrogation?" I asked carefully, knowing that the subject of the investigation must have been hard on him.

"It was… tough," Ethan sighed. "I didn't even get why I was there. I would never hurt my own sister."

I bit my lip, the stress of trying to find something to answer with paining me. "Need some company?"

As if it were bad to say yes, he slowly nodded, looking almost embarrassed.

I walked across the stone path and up the steps, where I took a seat next to him. "You know that if there's ever anything, you can always ask. I'm here if you need to talk or just want company."

"I thought I was just the pain in the ass," Ethan stated with a small laugh.

For a second, my heart stopped beating, and my smile faded. "No, you're more than just that, and you should know that. Hell, I wouldn't be the same if you weren't in my life. You both made me who I am today." It was silent for a minute until I looked over at the sheet in his hands. "What's that?"

"I found it in the back of Anna's phone case. You know how she used to always hide things in there, like extra cash and her school ID? Well, I decided to look this afternoon just in case there was something important, and behind a twenty-dollar bill, I found this." He handed over the wrinkled paper, which I began to read to myself.

> *She's the girl*
> *who runs with the wind in her face,*
> *conquering any situation*
> *with bravery no matter the case.*

> *She's the girl*
> *who dances under the glow of the late afternoon sun,*
> *making every difficult day*
> *into a time so fun.*

> *She's the girl*
> *who sings in the pouring rain,*
> *not making one single moment*
> *ever feel the same.*

> *She's the girl*
> *who jumps into life,*
> *taking the risky road*
> *to bring darkness into light.*

I was speechless.

"I remember hearing her whispering to herself at night, writing this as a school assignment. She's incredible, isn't she?"

"Yeah, no kidding. Have an idea who it's about?" I asked, staring down at it again, this time analyzing each word.

"I think it's about you."

His words felt like a blinding light being shined into my eyes. "Me?"

"Yeah, obviously. Who else runs into tricky situations, diving headfirst with bravery? Who makes everyday fun, no matter what happened before? Who likes to take the risky road?"

I blushed, that butterfly feeling fluttering in the pit of my stomach as he complimented me. After thinking about it for a second, though, I still couldn't believe it. "She would never say that I sing in the rain. I *hate* rain!" I laughed as I looked up at the sky. Lucky for me, it had stopped pouring by the time I had left the diner, and now, the sky was smudges of pinks and purples, forming a beautiful sunset.

"You're right about that, but I think it was the point that counted."

"She wrote it about me." It had started as a question, but it had ended as a statement.

She had written about *me*.

Her *best friend*.

I then spotted the time on Ethan's watch and began to stand up. "Shit, I've got to get going. My mom wanted me to get home by six o'clock." I held up the poem, the evening sunlight making the paper glow. "Mind if I keep it?"

Ethan nodded and stood up as I slipped the sheet into the side pocket of my coat. I then walked down the steps, and he followed me to the driveway.

"Call me, if you ever need anything," I told him, and before walking away, I briskly kissed his cheek, then crossed the street without saying a word.

Ethan Landers and I *weren't* a thing.

Nothing had ever happened between us.

We were *just friends.*

Growing up, he had only been that annoying sibling who would never leave me and Anna alone, as much as I *may* have enjoyed his company time-to-time. Though we got closer with age, I never allowed myself to see him as anything more – we were too different, and who knew how Anna would have reacted if I ever had tried something with him.

However, as I watched a smile curve upon his face, while his cheeks reddened, I knew that I had given Ethan one good memory on the tragic day.

My family's small, Cape-Cod-style house was chillier than usual as I walked through its unlocked entrance door. It was quiet inside, though I could faintly hear the buzz of loud rock music coming from the upstairs bedroom of my older brother, Caleb. A feeling of loneliness then crashed over me like a wave as I took off my black waterproof trench coat and hung it up in the entrance closet. The familiar smell of barbeque pulled pork hit my nose, and I suddenly gained an appetite.

After walking into the kitchen and peeking into the slow cooker to check on supper, I found a scrap piece of paper next to the barbeque sauce, written in my mom's loopy handwriting.

Had some errands to do. Will be back soon.

Of course, she had something else to do, I thought as I wandered into the living room.

The television screen was on, and though it was muted, I instantly recognized that *NCIS* was playing. I wasn't able to concentrate on the show in front of me, though, so I shut the TV off and jogged up the stairs to the second floor. I then entered the bathroom and slammed the door shut behind me.

Leaning over the bathtub to turn on the water, intent on taking a shower, more thoughts clouded my head. They started to drive me insane, and all I wanted to do was shake out my thoughts as if they were coins stuck in a piggy bank, as impossible as the task was.

However, that was when I turned the shower head on, and instead of steaming water showering down into the tub, I watched as hot blood gushed out. I almost screamed as memories from the night before flooded my mind–

I blinked, tears coming to my eyes, and suddenly, it was gone. There was no residue of blood – it was as if it had never   happened. There   were   just water droplets accumulating on the walls of the shower.

I dropped to the side of the tub, clutching the damp, dark gray shower curtain.

I'm a monster. I'm a fucking monster, I kept telling myself, unable to look at my reflection in the mirror.

I couldn't believe how much my life had changed in the past day, and how much it had started to scare me. Growing up, I had always thought that the worst feeling in the entire world was losing someone, but now I realized how mistaken I had been. The worst feeling was the emptiness you felt when you realized that you lost yourself and didn't know if you'd ever get the old you back.

I must think of something.

I can't get caught.

Feeling dizzy and sensing a headache coming on, I pulled myself up from the floor. I felt a sudden urge to take a painkiller, needing relief from my bottled-up agony. I began rummaging through the medicine cabinets until I found the aspirin bottle and popped two pills into my mouth, gulping them down without water.

As I closed the cabinet door, though, I came across the mirror smudged with blood, the words "I KNOW YOU DID IT" written in messy letters.

I almost shrieked until it vanished in another blink of an eye.

"You'll think of something," that same taunting voice said, surprisingly calming me down, instead of scaring me.

"Yeah, I'll think of something," I murmured to myself, the words slightly echoing off the walls.

Because nobody could ever find out about what I did.

This was only my and Annabeth's little secret to keep.

Chapter 4
Jessi
Loving You is a Losing Game

Some people didn't believe that Ouija boards *actually* worked – but *I* did.

At this point, a Ouija board felt like it was the only thing that would give us a chance at figuring out – or at least getting closer to figuring out – who Annabeth's killer was.

And to hopefully get to see her again, some part of me whispered, but I ignored the thought.

I had waited three weeks for my dad to get out of the house so that I could have it to myself – I was not ready to chance him walking into a séance. Though it was the night before the funeral, my dad was working late with a client, and it was now or never.

My house was a small bungalow, so since I wasn't wanting to use my bedroom, I was stuck using either the upstairs floor or the basement. The basement won since it had no windows and would be safest if a bad spirit broke any, but some part of me still kept saying that this was beginning to seem like the start of a bad horror movie.

I laid out a red-and-white plaid picnic blanket on the cold, hardwood floor and put the Ouija board box on top of it, though I didn't open it yet. I may have been the one who was going to lead the ritual, but that didn't make me any less nervous about it.

I then flopped onto the old, green-and-blue paisley-patterned couch on the other side of the room and sighed, fiddling with the charm bracelet that dangled from my right wrist. I had accumulated a decent collection of charms over the years, but some of them meant more to me than others. One was the small, bright blue ukulele charm – a near-perfect replica of my instrument – that Anna had given me for my fifteenth birthday. Tracing the familiar shape of the tiny ukulele, I felt a wave of sadness crash over me.

God, Anna, there's so much I never got to tell you...

I let the charm fall from my fingers as I picked at a stray thread from the couch and flipped absentmindedly through the photos in an album that had been left behind on the cushions. My dad was the type who liked to document *everything* through photos, and we had an *entire* bookshelf in the basement full of photo albums. Every holiday, school event, and volleyball tournament that I had ever participated in was labeled with the date, a title, and placed in chronological order.

The easy happiness in all of the photos – the innocence in them – made a tidal wave of pain wash over me. I knew that we would never be able to feel that happy ever again.

I slammed the photo album shut and threw it to the

other side of the couch with more aggression than it deserved.

I *had* to figure out who had killed Anna.

It was the least that I could do.

This will work, I promised myself for the billionth time. I glanced at the beige box in front of me, suddenly feeling nervous. *It'll work, and this will have all been worth it.*

I looked over at Adley, who had been sitting quietly on the floor since she had gotten to my house. She was intensely reading a wrinkled piece of paper, pausing every now and then with a thoughtful expression on her face.

I then suddenly had the urge to see it for myself. So, pretending to rearrange the flickering candles that I had set out on the little table behind Adley, I leaned as close as I dared and scanned the sheet that she was holding.

> *She's the girl*
> *who runs with the wind in her face,*
> *conquering any situation*
> *with bravery no matter the case.*
>
> *She's the girl*
> *who dances under the glow of the late afternoon sun,*
> *making every difficult day*
> *into a time so fun.*
>
> *She's the girl*
> *who sings in the pouring rain,*
> *not making one single moment*

ever feel the same.

She's the girl
who jumps into life,
taking the risky road
to bring darkness into light.

I immediately recognized Annabeth's neat, loopy handwriting and signature purple ink. I gasped, shocked since I had never known that she wrote poems – and this one was *amazing*.

Quickly looking away from the paper, afraid to be caught by Adley, I continued to rearrange the candles.

Okay, so Anna wrote poems, I thought. *But who's that one about?*

A lot of it seemed to be about Adley – the running since she was on the track team; the dancing since she used to take dance classes; the risky road thing since everyone knew how crazy she could be at times.

However, the part about singing in the rain? That *couldn't* be about Adley. She despised rain with a passion.

Could that part be... about me?

Suddenly, Adley whirled around, narrowing her brown eyes at me and crumpling the paper in her hand. "What are *you* looking at?"

"Nothing, nothing," I stammered, trying to act like I was rearranging my candles but knocking over a picture frame – one with a photo of me and Anna the morning of one of our volleyball games – in my panic. "Just, um, fixing the candles."

Adley shot me an unconvinced look but didn't add anything more. I let out a relieved breath, then returned to my spot on the floor, telling myself to focus on what Adley and I were here for.

Figuring out who had ruined *everything.*

I looked back over at Adley, and she was staring at the Ouija board box on the floor warily, twisting a strand of her dark blonde hair around her finger so tightly that the tip of her finger had gone white.

She was Anna's best friend too, I reminded myself, trying to ignore the uncomfortable feeling in my chest. *She's just nervous.*

I scooted over to Adley and put a hand on her bare arm, which was covered in goosebumps, making her jump. "Everything okay?"

"You know this might not work, right, Jess?" she started, sighing. "This could go wrong, and–"

I waved a hand, shushing her. "You can't start this off thinking so negatively. We are *going* to figure this out, no matter what."

Without giving her a chance to argue, I took my place across from her and in front of the Ouija board box. The box itself was nothing special, just beige cardboard with "Ouija" printed on it in its signature font, but I still felt nervous looking at it. With a deep breath, I pulled off the top of the box and reached inside for the board, laying it and its planchette on the blanket.

Adley leaned forward, peering into the box, then cautiously pulled the rulebook out. Her eyes scanned the yellowed paper, and I could see the color draining from her face. Admittedly, the first time that I read the rulebook, I had been terrified too.

"*Never play alone,*" she recited. "*Never play in a graveyard or where someone has died.*" Adley looked into my eyes, frowning. "This is some pretty creepy shit, Jess."

"Creepy, yes," I admitted. "But crap? No. If you don't follow those rules, it won't end well."

Adley rolled her eyes, but her fear showed through her façade. "*Whatever.* Can we just do this?"

I took the planchette in my hands and laid it on the board. Then, I pressed my index finger to its center, motioning for Adley to copy me. We passed it in a circle along the perimeter of the board a few times to warm it up.

"Annabeth," I began, making sure that my voice was loud and clear. "Annabeth Landers, are you here?"

Adley and I held our breath, sitting stiff and still—

Nothing.

Another minute passed.

Still nothing.

"See?" Adley boasted, looking almost relieved. "It's all *fake*—" She choked on her words as the pointer started to move.

It slowly made its way across the lavishly patterned board and landed on the section on the top-left-hand side of the board labeled YES. Then, it returned to its original spot in the center of the board.

"It's her," I whispered, and Adley looked both doubtful and terrified all at once.

Okay, I thought, willing myself not to get too

excited. *Maybe this* isn't *Anna. I'll only know by asking her something that only she'd know.*

"Now, what was the worst mark that you had ever gotten in history class?"

Anna had always gotten good grades in school, but for some reason, she had struggled with history. The two of us had started studying together after she had failed her ninth-grade mid-term, but Anna hadn't told *anyone* else about her bad grade.

It had been nice to feel so trusted by her.

I caught Adley's eye, and she raised an eyebrow at me. "Seriously? She'd never remember that," Adley whispered.

Just as I was about to snap back and say that Anna always remembered the little things, the pointer glided toward the number section on the board. I glanced at the number it had landed on, making a mental note of it, then watched intently as it landed on the next. "Forty-seven," I murmured – close, but not close enough.

Of course, it wouldn't have been that easy.

I opened my mouth to tell Adley to pull the pointer toward GOODBYE, but suddenly, it started to move again. "And... a... half," I spelled out, a smile creeping up my face.

I can't believe it. I can't believe *it.*

"It's her," I told Adley. "Only *she* would know that specific number."

Adley didn't respond, having gone whiter than a sheet and looking as if she wanted to yank her hands off the planchette and run away.

I looked back at the board, suddenly feeling nervous.

Go, It's really her. *What do I* say?

"Anna," I choked. "I can't believe it's you. I mean, of course, it's you. Who else would it *be–*"

"Should you really be *talking*?" Adley snapped. "That seems like a stupid idea. Maybe we should just *stop–*"

"Be quiet, Adley! I'm trying to *think–*" I cut myself off, remembering a vital detail: If I looked through the glass window of the planchette, I would be able to *see* Anna. I looked at Adley, feeling excitement rise in my chest. "Adley, we can *see* her! If we look through the little window, we can–"

Before I had the chance to finish my sentence or pick the planchette up, Adley yanked it from my grip like it was a stray fifty-dollar bill that she had found on the curb. She held it up to her face, staring through the glass circle with one eye. "Shit!" she said softly, less like a whisper and more like a muted cry of fear. She looked, quite honestly, like she had seen a ghost.

So, maybe she *had*.

I went to grab the planchette, but before I could, Adley slammed it back onto the board. She yanked the pointer toward GOODBYE, lifted it off the board, and snapped it in half.

Adley had just stolen the one chance I had to see Annabeth.

I'm never going to see her again.

Anger thrumming through my body, I whirled on Adley. "What the hell, Adley? You just ruined *everything*! Do you even care–"

"You don't get it," she yelled back in frustration,

leaving me speechless. Making a fist around the broken pieces, she then ran off, stumbling up the stairs and disappearing along with the only chance I had at finding out who had ruined our lives.

Chapter 5
Adley
The Secrets We Bury

The Landers family was waiting at the entrance of the Ember Falls town church, greeting everyone in their formal outfits as the guests arrived for Annabeth's funeral.

Stepping out of my brother's BMW, I spotted Ethan, dressed in a pair of dress pants and a polo shirt, both the color of death. He was standing silently next to his family, staring down at the grass beneath him. Once I approached them, alongside my mother and Caleb, Ethan glanced up with a small smile.

"God, I'm so sorry, man. Your sister deserved better," Caleb said first, cutting in front of me and hugging Ethan.

"Thanks. I'm happy that you guys were able to come," Ethan answered, and as I placed a hand on his shoulder supportively, I felt how stiff and cold his body was.

"Of course, we wouldn't miss it for anything," I reminded Ethan, my smile sad.

Caleb then waved quickly to Ethan's parents before ducking into the church with my mother, though I stayed back with Ethan.

"You look really nice," he commented, and I felt myself blush despite everything. I looked down at my long, black cross-neck dress and black heels, then tucked a curl nervously behind my ear. Before I was able to say thanks, though, he added, "But, um, are you okay? You're *shivering*."

"I'm fine. It's just a little chilly." I rubbed my bare arms with my hands, when suddenly, Ethan pulled off his black jacket and draped it over my shoulders.

"Here," he whispered, and I smiled at him, the warmth of his jacket making me feel better instantly.

That was when I heard footsteps behind me and turned to see Jessi in her way-too-vibrant, blue-and-pink, floral-patterned, A-line scoop dress. Being herself, she believed that wearing something bright and colorful instead of sad and dark would celebrate life, instead of saying goodbye to it. I wasn't sure if it was a superstition or not, as there was *always* an excuse with her, but I kept my mouth shut. I was too drained to judge. After all, she surprisingly *did* look nice – besides the fact that she was wearing her white, grass-stained *sneakers*.

Without words, Jessi hugged Ethan, and a tight sensation bloomed in my ribcage, almost as if someone were squeezing my heart. I had a strange urge to get her away from him, but then, she stepped away before I could think anything of it.

"Hey, can I go in and take a seat now?" Ethan asked his parents, turning to meet their gazes.

Mrs. Landers nodded, a faint smile on her lips. Before Ethan or I could step into the old, white building, Jessi slipped past us and entered the musty interior. Ethan and I followed into the high-ceilinged church hall that was filled with rows of chipped wooden benches. Its walls were embedded with large stain-glass windows, allowing the hot rays of sun to pour into the dark room.

Ethan pulled me and Jessi into the front row, which was reserved for family members. "Can you guys sit with me?" he asked, his eyes filled with hope.

Jessi and I nodded, knowing that we couldn't leave him at a time like this. I sat down next to the aisle, Ethan sandwiched between me and Jessi. Then, uncomfortably, we stared ahead at the empty stage, not saying a word.

It wasn't usually like this when we were together, but without Anna, *nothing* was the same. Especially after the summoning ritual that Jessi and I had performed the night before, which we had both sworn not to tell Ethan about. It would have only hurt him more.

And, hell, I was *scared.* One more moment of playing would have revealed the cold, hard truth about the night of Anna's death.

I knew that the game wasn't fake.

I had *seen* her.

I had seen *Annabeth*, dressed in her purple, spaghetti-strapped nightgown, and golden locks perfectly curled.

At least, I had seen her ghost through the planchette's glass hole, if that had even been possible, and my mind hadn't just been playing tricks on me.

It had to have been that, though – just *tricks*. Ghosts didn't *actually* exist–

I snapped back into reality as Ethan's knee touched mine. He briskly looked me in the eye, but we didn't speak, even though I knew that he must have sensed my nerves.

Ethan's parents then walked down the church's narrow aisle and up the steps of the small stage. Anna's black casket and enlarged memorial picture were presented there, which only made everything feel so much more real.

Anna really was *dead.*

Throughout the presentation, the audience was peacefully silent. Only a few people whimpered softly, trying not to cry, while reliving the memories with everyone.

After a couple of speeches were performed, only my speech was left to be presented. When Mrs. Landers announced my name, I felt all eyes on me. I gave Ethan his jacket back, then slowly got up from my spot and made my way onto the stage, in front of the podium.

I wasn't the nervous type, but now my stomach was turning in circles like a hypnosis wheel. I could easily hear my heartbeat thump rapidly in my chest. Beginning to sweat as my thoughts raced, making my mind blank, I decided to fish out the folded, wrinkled napkin that I had shoved into the pocket of my Kate Spade purse. I never planned out things since I preferred speaking on the spot, which stressed me less, but I couldn't risk screwing everything up.

I gripped the napkin and tried to read out the points that I had made the night before. I had known that something like this was bound to happen when all I wanted to do was scream, "I killed her."

"Hi," I began, absentmindedly twirling a loose curl. My eyes then fell quickly on Ethan, who smiled encouragingly at me. I fidgeted with the napkin and licked my dry lips. *"God,* I don't even know where to start." Everyone in the audience laughed tearfully, which motivated me to go on. "I'd like to start by thanking all of you for coming in honor of my best friend. Annabeth Landers was a goddess. She did everything with such power and authenticity, and she truly was a role model who had her entire life planned out. She also gave amazing advice as if she were a vending machine of wisdom." That made me laugh, though I tried to hold it in, not wanting to falter. "I remember the time that I was watching my first horror movie with Anna. Twelve-year-old me was crying over the death of Jenna in the *Friday the 13th* remake. But Anna then told me, 'It's hard to keep watching when you know someone won't be in the next scene, but the story must go on.' Even though we *aren't* in a horror movie, I think that now is the time that we need to remember that. Especially since our favorite character has been removed from our stories. I think Anna would have wanted us to enjoy life for her, even if she couldn't anymore."

A tear slipped from my eye as I heard that little voice in the back of my head whisper, *"And that's all because of you."*

After the organ played, announcing that the ceremony was ending, everyone stood up silently, still wiping away tears. Mr. and Mrs. Landers led all the guests out of the church, while a few family members volunteered to carry the casket.

Once my and Ethan's row exited the church to go outside, we circled the casket, which had been placed down on a patch of perfectly green grass, next to a deep rectangular-shaped hole in the ground. Then, shifting uncomfortably during the process, I watched as the casket was lowered into the hole that seemed to never end. Some part of me wanted to exchange places with her since she had no reason to be in that position.

But she was dead, and I couldn't bring her back to life.

As if the world wanted me to feel guiltier, everyone close to Anna was then given a chance to throw a shovelful of dirt onto the coffin. As I threw my shovelful of dirt, I felt as if I had killed her all over again. I was barely able to do it – my vision was, once again, bombarded with flashes of blood and Anna's limp body.

Then, after a moment of silence and another speech from the Landers family, everyone broke off into groups. The guests either took a walk around the cemetery grounds for a change of air or attacked the small food buffet that had been set up.

I, on the other hand, advanced closer to the odd-shaped, gray stone that stood at the top of Anna's grave like a headboard of a bed.

Or more accurately, a halo above an angel's head.

Annabeth Eloise Landers
Loving Friend and Daughter
July 23rd, 1999 – August 2nd, 2015

A single tear ran down the side of my cheek as Ethan joined me, his eyes wide with shock. "As much as we want her back, Adley, you know that's not how life works," he told me, resting a hand on my shoulder. "She's in a good place."

"Yeah, she is." I stepped back, glanced at the stone one more time, and walked away. I decided to head for the buffet, where I quickly snuck a glass of champagne off the table.

Just as I began sprinting down one of the rocky cemetery paths, though, I ran straight into a body. The bubbly liquid in my cup sloshed around, almost spilling onto the pebbles beneath me.

I looked up from my glass to find Jessi staring at me with the scary eyes she barely wore, which then fell upon my drink. "You're trying to sneak a drink at a moment like *this*?"

"One glass isn't going to get me drunk, Miss Perfect." I shoved past her and sat on the hot, ceramic bench in front of me.

"We need to talk," Jessi insisted, as she sat down beside me. I resisted another eye roll.

"Okay, sure. What about?" I took a sip of my champagne, crossing a leg over the other.

"Yesterday. What happened? And please don't come up with a foolish lie like, 'It was nothing', because we both know it *wasn't*."

"I was just under a lot of stress," I confessed, which *was* true – when a haunting voice kept commanding you to stop the entire time, you couldn't think straight. "Just thinking of maybe seeing Anna brought back memories, and it scared me. You have to understand what I mean."

"So, you *didn't* see Anna through the planchette's window?"

I took another sip from my glass, needing time to think about what to reply with. I couldn't tell her the truth – I knew that things would smooth out a lot more easily if I just lied. "No, it was pretty much one of those cheap-ass magnifying glasses from the Dollar Tree that never work. The whole thing was a *scam*, Jess."

"But breaking the planchette? What was *that* for?"

Damn Jessi and her never-ending questions.

"You know me. When I'm pissed off or insanely anxious, I tend to do a lot of stupid things that I don't think about until I've already done them."

"Like knocking back that drink?" Jessi asked, her dark eyes zeroing in on my glass.

I looked down at the empty champagne flute held in my right hand. "Nah, I don't regret a thing about that. I barely felt it," I laughed, tossing a lock of hair out of my face. "Look, I know that it was your only chance to find out–"

"Forget about it," Jessi snapped, her words rushed and slightly harsh in annoyance. "I've brainstormed another way to discover the truth anyway."

I choked on my saliva. "Y-You *did*?"

I didn't get it – why couldn't she just leave the investigation up to the police? Why couldn't she just not wedge her nose into matters that did not concern her?

"Yeah, I'm going to do a little sleuthing of my own. I'm just gonna ask around and see if anybody knows something that can help us find Anna's killer. You look shocked." Jessi's eyebrows furrowed as she analyzed my reaction.

I hadn't even noticed that I had let my expression change at all. "No, I'm not shocked."

Jessi smiled triumphantly, but it scared me more than ever. "Did you really think that I *didn't* have a Plan B?"

The sky was dark blue and mystifying, and the sparkling specks of stars were the only source of light on the depressing, chilly evening. I wrapped my bare arms around myself, trying to keep warm.

The roof of my house was flat at the top, making it easy to sit up there for hours and watch the stars. I did it quite often – not for the stars, but so that I could have a private drinking spot when my parents weren't home. It usually calmed me down when I felt stressed about something.

"Want my sweater?"

I sat up and looked over at Ethan, who was carefully walking across the roof's tiles after climbing up the ladder. He looked nervous, holding his hands out for balance, while he stepped cautiously with his knees bent.

"What are you doing here?" I asked instead, laughing. "You aren't one to do this."

He shrugged before taking a seat next to me and throwing his baggy, navy-blue sweater my way. I pulled it on without arguing. "I saw you from my window – not that I was watching you, because I'm not some kind of stalker – but I was worried about you and thought that you might need some company." His chocolate-brown eyes were full of tears as he added, "I'm sorry again about your dad."

"Me too," I thought aloud, as I took a sip from the can of beer that I had robbed from the fridge. "Maybe one day, we'll find out what had actually happened to him – 'going missing' is no explanation."

"Are you planning on solving another mystery, Nancy Drew?" Ethan cocked an eyebrow my way, and I elbowed him playfully.

"No, solving crime isn't my thing. Besides, I don't even think I want to know how my father died." I took another sip from my can, then looked back up at Ethan, who was empty-handed. "Oh, do you want one?" He looked hesitant for a second, but I didn't let him reply. Sometimes, Ethan just had to loosen up a bit. "Take a sip of mine." I shoved the cold, metal can in his face, and he reluctantly took it.

"Ew, this tastes nasty!" he cried after taking a sip, spitting the liquid out.

"And it does the trick," I replied, as I ripped the can out of his hands and knocked back the last few mouthfuls. "Remind me why you are here instead of Anna?" I prompted after a minute of awkward silence.

Ethan looked away from my eyes and lay down on the roof, looking up at the stars. I placed my can down beside me and did the same, my head resting on top of his shoulder. "Because Anna is too busy going out on her date with this week's boyfriend. Because I care to check up on you. Because I love you."

I let out a small giggle. "I love you too, E, but I think you're being a little dramatic. She's just out having fun. Anna still loves me just as much as you do."

"Does she? After what you did to her, I wouldn't blame her for hating you."

I blinked and rapidly sat up, confused.

The sky was still dark. I was still on top of my roof, though I was now dressed in my black cocktail dress, and no sweater was warming my arms. An empty beer can still rolled in the wind like a tumbleweed.

However, Ethan was gone.

Well, he was replaced by a tall guy with messy, dark chestnut-brown hair and stunning cheekbones.

I must be drunk, I thought as I leaned closer to him and tried touching his hand to see if I was hallucinating. It was soft and one hundred percent *real.*

"Oh, I see where we're going with this–"

"Who *are* you?" I bit back, pulling away from him, my body trembling.

"You don't recognize me?" he gasped, his eyes wide.

He wasn't from school, for sure, and neither was he a police officer from the investigation – he looked more as if he was in his early twenties. His appearance barely reminded me of anyone I knew, but his voice sounded so familiar – so natural – as if it was engraved in my brain.

"What's your name?" I questioned, frustrated that I wasn't recognizing him.

He sat up and scooted over so that he was close enough for me to smell his overpowering cologne. "The name's Damion."

"So, um, Damion," I continued, trying to think about what to say next. "If you really know me, what's *my* name?"

He barely even took a second to think that question through. "Adley Morgenstern."

My heart leaped at the sound of my name, and I glanced around the yard to see if anyone was secretly spying. "What's going on? Please tell me this is a *joke*."

"Relax. I'm just so happy that you can *finally* see me after all these years." He tried to touch my hand with his, which I just slapped.

"What's *wrong* with you, psychopath?" I screamed as I stood up and grabbed my beer can quickly. I scampered over to the shed's roof, which I landed on before climbing down the ladder.

The man chased after me in his all-black outfit as I ran across the vacant yard, trying to make it to the small patio deck. "Look, I'm sorry if I'm coming off *a little* strong. I know that you just came from Annabeth's funeral, but I didn't think you'd be as sensitive as everyone else. You *were* the one who killed her, after all."

I had been about halfway up the patio's steps but froze in place at the words that escaped his mouth.

Only two people knew what had *really* happened that night – at least that was what I had thought.

How does this strange man know?

"What are you *saying*?" I asked the man, panic in my voice.

"I'm saying that you *must* know me. Come on, A. We're friends, maybe even *family*."

His voice, *his voice*–

Suddenly, it hit me.

He's the one – the one who's been whispering in my

ear for years…

"And I know *all* your secrets."

"I… *believe* you," I admitted as I looked up at the bright, yellow-white moon in the clear sky.

I *did* recognize him.

He was who belonged to the voice that had persuaded me to kill my best friend.

Chapter 6
Jessi
I Knew You Were Trouble

"Just shut up*! Leave me* alone*!" I shouted the same plea into the darkness over and over, trying to get the voice to quiet down and leave me in peace.*

"Don't try. You'll only get hurt."

"Stop!" I cried, pressing my hands over my ears, attempting to block out the voice and failing.

"Failure comes at a steep cost, Jessi."

"Stop it!" I screamed, but the voice only got louder. "Please, just stop!"

"Failure comes at a steep cost–"

I jolted awake, disoriented, and tangled in my sheets.

Ever since Anna had died, I had been having these strange, feverish dreams. Some nights it was threats, some nights it was pleas, and some nights it was an odd clash of the two. The voice wasn't recognizable and was accented ever so slightly, having a bizarre, echoey quality as if someone was talking to me from far away.

I wasn't sure what to make of it.

It was just a dream, I told myself, rubbing my eyes. *Just an imaginary voice.*

As I got out of bed, I spotted my ukulele in its spot next to my desk, then suddenly felt sad. Playing it was the one thing I knew that I could do well, and I had always imagined getting to play something for Anna one day.

Tearing my eyes away from the small instrument, I slowly walked out of my room and into the bathroom, still hearing the echoey voice in my head. I leaned forward against the marble bathroom counter, looking at myself in my still-sleepy, brown eyes.

"It was just a dream," I firmly told my reflection as if it might argue back. "Just a stupid dream."

But the creepy voice still echoed in the back of my mind, repeating its threat.

Don't try. You'll only get hurt. Failure comes at a steep cost, Jessi.

I shook my head, banishing the voice to the recesses of my mind. *No, I'm not going to give up. I'm going to try.*

Maybe I would get hurt, but it would be worth it. I was *going* to find Annabeth's killer, no matter what my subconscious told me.

A newfound determination edging me on, I headed upstairs and wandered into the kitchen, where my dad was rushing around like a maniac. Standing in the doorway, I watched as he nearly spilled a carafe of hot coffee on himself. I then heard him mumble angrily at the coffee machine in Spanish.

My grandparents had grown up in Mexico, and even though my dad had been born in Ember Falls, they had made sure that he knew both English and Spanish. I was also fluent in both languages, which was why I couldn't help but giggle at the ridiculous things my dad was saying to the coffee machine.

"So," I started, "may I ask what's going on?"

"No 'good morning'?" my dad laughed, putting the carafe back on the counter. Then, he sighed, rubbing a hand across his face. "A client called. I need to go and help them out with a case. I know I was supposed to be free—"

"It's fine, *Papi*," I interrupted. "Adley and I were thinking that we might hang out today, anyway."

Or I'll investigate my best friend's murder. One or the other.

My dad seemed relieved that I wouldn't be spending the entire day alone. He checked his watch, grabbed his briefcase, then hurriedly tied his shoes. "Bye, *Mija*," he said, kissing me on the head, and I waved goodbye as he rushed out the door.

Once I was sure that my dad's car was gone, I went and put on my grass-stained, white sneakers, planning my trajectory for the day. First, I would see Ethan — I didn't suspect him of his own twin's murder, but I had a strong feeling that he could give me some leads. Then, as much as it pained me to think about it, I would find Drake Rachford, Annabeth's most recent boyfriend — not that I suspected him either, but he'd had close ties to Anna.

By then, I hoped that I would have a few other people in mind to whom I could talk to. I wasn't sure if my plan would get me anywhere, but I had to try.

Climbing onto my second-hand, ocean-blue bike, I tried to imagine ways that I could cut my conversation with Drake as short as possible, then mentally scolded myself for being so bitter. After everything, Drake didn't deserve that anger – not from me, anyway.

Determinedly, I headed in the direction of the Landers' house, trying not to think of how Ethan had looked the last time that I had seen him. I had talked to him a bit at the funeral, and he had seemed so *broken.*

That's why I'm doing this, I reminded myself. *It's the least that I can do for Ethan.*

I sighed, suddenly thinking back to everything that had happened with the Ouija board the other day. Had it even worked? I had been so sure that it would, but Adley had denied that without so much as a second thought.

Unless Adley lied.

I shook my head. Why would she have lied? Maybe Adley had things to hide, but Anna had been her friend too.

So, why did she freak out so badly?

It had to have been out of shock – a spur-of-the-moment decision.

Those are *Adley's specialty,* I thought bitterly. *But something still doesn't feel quite right–*

I was so caught up in my thoughts that I hadn't realized that, even though I had ridden down the Landers' street, I had wound up at *Adley's* house. Part of me was tempted to go and ring the doorbell like old times, but another part of me said that it probably wasn't such a good idea. After everything that had gone down with Adley and the Ouija board, I wasn't exactly sure that she *wanted* to be part of this investigation at all.

And, if I was being honest with myself, I didn't want to see whatever hungover mess she had surely turned herself into after the funeral the day before. I knew Adley well enough to know that the glass of champagne that she had drunk at the funeral wouldn't have been her last drink of the day.

Tearing my gaze away from Adley's familiar front door, I headed toward the Landers' big, Victorian house. After parking my bike in the driveway, I slowly made my way up the porch stairs, biting the scab on my lip. Tentatively, I reached up and rang the doorbell.

Is it too early? I tended to get up earlier than other people my age, and I hadn't checked the time before I had left my house. *God, I would feel so bad if I woke someone up–*

The door creaked open, and Ethan poked his head out. Thankfully, he seemed completely awake, a smile on his face as he opened the door. "Hey, Jessi. What brings you here at" –Ethan checked his watch– "8:50 in the morning?"

"Oh. Is it *that* early?" I blushed, embarrassed as I looked down at the ground. "I'm sorry. I can come back later–"

He shook his head. "It's fine, I've been up for a while. I was about to head out, actually."

"Where to?" I asked, trying to start a conversation before I dropped the I'm-Searching-for-your-Sister's-Murderer bombshell.

Ethan shrugged. "Somewhere away from the house. It feels kind of suffocating in there, you know?" I nodded, so he added, "But back to my original question: What are you doing here so early?"

"Oh, right," I said, trying not to imagine his reaction to what I was about to say next. "I was, um… wondering if you had any ideas of people that I could talk to?" Ethan cocked his head to the side, waiting for me to clarify. "You know… about Anna."

He looked dazed for a second as if hearing his sister's name had physically hurt him. Then, he took a deep breath and looked at the floor. "About *Anna*?"

"Yeah," I replied, feeling bad that I had asked. "I'm looking into, you know…" Judging by the sad look on Ethan's face and the dark circles under his eyes, I knew that I wasn't going to be able to tell him the full truth – I would have to make up a believable story. "I was just wanting to make a memoir of sorts. Nothing big. Just for myself."

Ethan's expression softened as he looked up from the floor and back at me. "Yeah," he said quietly. "Yeah, I'm sure I could find you some people." He blew out his breath and raked a hand through his blond hair. "For starters, I'd suggest Drake, and you could always talk to Kristen Decker, Anna's old friend from the lacrosse team. Or anyone from the volleyball team."

I nodded, trying not to seem annoyed. This whole conversation was getting me *nowhere.*

"And… Oh, yeah, I remember Anna mentioning this girl… Ivy Blackthorn, was it? I think they hung out once or twice."

Ivy? I stiffened and started to pay closer attention to what Ethan had to say.

"I mean, they didn't seem very close," Ethan continued, oblivious to my shock. "Ivy seemed a bit intense, especially from what I heard from Anna. Anyway, this list is just off the top of my head." He shrugged. "Ivy's probably not a great resource for something like a memoir. I think she's in Paris, anyhow."

I knew that she *wasn't*, but I nodded, forcing a grin. "Thanks." Without adding anything more, I made my way down the stairs, willing my legs not to shake.

Then, I climbed onto my bike and took off, my mind racing. I knew that Adley had hung around Ivy in the past — she had left me and Anna for the second half of ninth year to hang out with Ivy and Nate, Adley's ex-boyfriend. Plus, once Nate had left for New York, Ivy and Adley had gotten even closer during tenth grade.

But *Annabeth*? She had never hung around with Ivy, as far as I had known. Anna had hated when Adley had abandoned her, and she had produced some very *colorful* words for Ivy and Nate.

Anna had never hung around with Ivy.

Unless she had, I thought, dread making my mouth taste sour. I gripped my handlebars harder.

If Annabeth had known Ivy, this investigation *was* going somewhere.

Ivy Blackthorn was now my first suspect.

Chapter 7

Adley

The Day I Tried to Live

Waking up the morning after the funeral, I felt wrecked.

I lay in my bed, my arms sprawled out so that I could touch every corner of my queen-sized bed, still restless from the chilly night that had just passed.

However, after everything, the only thing on my mind was Damion. I knew that I hadn't needed to be drunk to see him since I now saw his blurry shadow in the corner of my bedroom. I turned over in exhaustion.

"Good morning, A," his bitter voice called, sounding muffled due to the pillow I had pulled over my head.

I sat up slowly and began to fix the small strands of hair that stood up on my head. Then, I watched as Damion got up from the oak rocking chair in the corner of my room and came over to me. He sat down on the corner of the bed that wasn't against one of my light gray walls.

"Why are you here?" I yawned, stretching my arms.

"A, I'm *always* here–"

"I know *that* already," I sighed, remembering what he had told me the night before — right before I had almost *lost my mind*. Apparently, he was tied to me in a way where he could communicate with me telepathically, though he was only now able to take physical form due to my recent "dark behavior." He was also able to appear and disappear whenever he pleased, though I was the only one who could hear and see him. "I *mean*," I continued, "why are you *here*?"

"Because I want to be? I think that it's better to see a visual than to only hear a voice–"

"Can you, like, *disappear*?" I shouted, frustration taking over. "Just for a while? I feel horrible right now and just want to get away from everything."

With that exclamation, I heard a soft notification tune from my iPhone, brightening up the screen and the area next to my bed. Once I opened the blinds, I walked over to my desk and looked at the message.

Ethan
9:02 AM
Hey!
I know it may be early for you
but I was wondering if you wanna do something.
Being at home is driving me crazy.

His message made me smile, and I closed my eyes, debating what to reply with. I hated mornings but knew that I couldn't stay here in my room, locked up with *Damion*. I was desperate, and besides, I couldn't stop living because Anna had.

My mind still hurt from everything that had happened – the murder, the funeral, the investigation, Damion – but I needed to get out just as much as Ethan did. So, with a smile on my face, I quickly replied and told him to pick me up at 9:30 AM, giving me just enough time to get ready.

"Ooh, is that your *boyfriend*?" Damion questioned, glancing over at my screen.

I shut off my phone so that he couldn't snoop, then stood up and walked toward my dresser. Opening the closet door, I rummaged through my clothes, looking for something perfect to fit the extremely hot temperature outside. I came upon a simple black tank top and a pair of comfortable denim shorts, then threw them onto my unmade bed.

"No, of course, not. He's Anna's *brother*, remember? We're *just* friends who want a break from reality."

"Who will spend lots of time together, I presume? After all, you're both in pain from the incident. It starts harmless, only being small hangouts until, soon enough, you need each other's company in more ways than you'd think–"

"All right, all right!" I cried, disturbed by the thought. I then motioned with my hand for Damion to turn around and stare at one of my boring walls as I pulled off my pajama top and put on my bra and shirt. "I *don't* like him, okay?" I continued as I put on the pair of clean shorts and finished by brushing out my dull hair. It was crusty from the products I had put in it the day before to make the flyaway hairs stay in place, so I decided to throw it up into a ponytail instead of leaving it loose like I usually did. "And I most certainly don't want him in *that way*."

Turning around and noticing that I was done changing but had just forgotten to tell him, Damion looked my way and let out a long, exasperated sigh. "*Okay*, then. But just remember, I *know* you. As much as you may be telling yourself things, it doesn't mean that they're always true."

Needing relief from another headache, I popped two aspirin in my mouth and swallowed them with a gulp of water from a glass in the kitchen.

However, just as I was heading toward the living room to watch TV, I caught my brother walking down the stairs in a vibrant, orange tank top. "Where are *you* going?"

"Baseball," he replied as he pointed to his Ember Falls Phoenix jersey – it reminded me so much of Anna's, though his jersey had the number "two" on it in gold, while hers had had the number "twenty-three". "It's the last game of the season. Are you coming to watch?"

My mom had already left for work, so I knew that I was the only person left that could cheer him on as he made a home run. *If* he made one, that was. I had never seen him play since it was his first year, and I had no interest in watching team sports – I preferred track and field.

Feeling sorry for him, I quickly changed my original answer. "*Fine*," I sighed. "It wasn't like Ethan and I had anything better to do."

"All right! I'll have my two favorite people cheering me on in the stands." Caleb hugged me before taking off toward the kitchen so that he could eat something for breakfast, and I felt myself smile ever so slightly.

"So, why were you so desperate to leave the house this time?" I asked Ethan as he entered the house, making his way into the kitchen where my brother sat at the kitchen island.

"Today, we received another three dishes of cabbage rolls," Ethan groaned, almost in disgust. "I know that everyone is sorry about what happened, but all my parents start to do is blame each other for everything. Then, they start arguing, and I just *can't* take it."

I could see his eyes water from his words, and I suddenly got an urge to hug him. However, I decided to take a seat with him at the dining room table instead. I knew that Ethan didn't want any more pity.

"Plus, something weird happened this morning."

"What?" my brother asked Ethan, butting into the conversation as he took another bite of Captain Crunch cereal. He then got off his stool and took a seat next to Ethan at the table.

"Jessi arrived at my door this morning, asking me for people that Anna knew. She said that she wanted to make 'a memoir of sorts.'"

"*What?*" I couldn't understand what had gotten into her, lying like that.

She just can't stop investigating for one day, can she?

"Yeah, she just came by for answers, then left. Honestly, it was weird seeing her so involved in something like this."

"Ditto," I mumbled under my breath.

That girl was either going to murder someone – or *be* killed by somebody – if that meant finding Anna's killer. I just couldn't understand *why.*

What was so *special* about Anna?

When it was ten o'clock, we rode in my brother's car to the small park a few streets down from our house. The recreational center was surprisingly packed – it was filled with kids on every play object in the park, players warming up in the small baseball field, and observers tackling the stands.

After wishing Caleb good luck, Ethan and I sprinted toward the bleachers and luckily found an available spot at the top of the stands.

"So, is this enough of a break from reality for you?" I asked, smiling over at Ethan.

"Yeah. It brings back a lot of good memories, which isn't such a terrible thing, I guess."

I nodded as I looked over at the swing set a few feet away, which Anna and I used to spend all our weekends on. We'd swing away and gossip together, while Ethan would play with his soccer ball in the nearby empty field, trying to kick it between the two rusted poles.

Thinking back to those times, I felt a little bit guilty for always leaving Ethan alone. I would have hated him if he had been like that with me.

"Why do you like me?" I blurted, and I caught his eyes widening in shock. "Why do you still want to spend time with me after I treated you so badly growing up?"

Ethan sat silently, wringing his hands in his lap. "There's just something about you," he said, trying to find the words. "Even though you always followed in Anna's footsteps, it didn't mean that you were a bad person." He looked up into my eyes as I stared into his.

"But we had *always* left you alone."

He laughed. "*Anna* had always left me alone because I was her annoying brother, and you looked up to her, Adley. It was easy to tell."

I blushed, feeling a little embarrassed. I had looked up to her a lot – she had been the kind of person that every girl wanted to be, and every guy wanted to be with. Maybe it was because Anna had made me feel like I wasn't alone in this scary world, or maybe it was because she had easily turned me into her clone, but I always wanted to *be* her.

At least, that was until I *had* become like her and had lost myself.

"But, anyway, that was the past," Ethan said with a small smile. "I'm happy that we can rely on each other and be friends now."

That was when the game started, the whole crowd cheering as my brother came out to bat first. As he made it to first base, though, Ethan touched my hand. I felt a tingly sensation climb up my back as my heartbeat sped up, and the only thing that crossed my mind was Damion and his disturbing words.

It starts harmless, only being small hangouts until, soon enough, you need each other's company in more ways than you'd think.

"Hey, do you want popcorn? I can get some," I stated, letting go of Ethan's hand as my mind started to race. I couldn't tell if I was happy or scared about his gesture but knew for sure that I needed space to think.

He looked taken aback. "Um, sure. You can get us a bag from the vendor."

"You know what? I'll get us *both* one!" I exclaimed, getting up in a rush and almost kicking the blonde woman who sat in front of us. I picked up my black, canvas strap tote bag as Ethan pulled me back down beside him.

"What's up with you?" he asked, concern lacing his voice.

"Nothing. Just headaches," I informed, and as if summoning the devil himself, I winced in pain at another headache. I pulled out an orange see-through pill bottle from my purse, then swallowed another two aspirin, this time without water.

"Are you okay? Do you wanna head home? I can walk you back—"

"E, all I want now is a bag of popcorn, okay?"

I knew that Ethan was realizing that something more was going on. And when he looked down at his hand, which was back on mine, I had a feeling that he realized what was up. I pulled my hand out of his possession as he remarked, "God, what's *wrong* with me? Am I making you uncomfortable? I just thought we were friends."

"We are!" I cried, standing back up. "We're friends who are here for each other because we're both in pain, but, soon enough, it's going to become *more*." I bit my bottom lip, looking away for a second. "I know it will, and I don't know if that's what I want." When Ethan didn't respond after a long moment, I stood up and stated, "I'm gonna get us some popcorn now."

I couldn't believe what had happened.

Standing in the long lineup as I waited to buy popcorn, I kept reflecting on the incident, which only made me feel worse.

Maybe I shouldn't have yelled. Was it a bad idea to mention what Damion had told me this morning? Did it only make things worse? I should have just kept my mouth shut...

But even I knew that everything about *us* was overwhelming me.

Come on, he's Anna's brother! *What was I thinking? He* may *like me, but he's probably not even thinking that far—*

"Yes?" an irritated voice asked.

Snapping out of my thoughts, I noticed a tall guy in a white apron, which was stained with what looked like melted butter. I was now at the front of the line underneath the blue tent, where the guy was selling food at a folding table, such as popcorn, cotton candy, chip bags, and water bottles.

"Can I have two bags of popcorn, please?" I asked politely, though the guy gave me a glare that made me wish that I had yelled out my order instead.

"Sorry, but we can only give you one bag of popcorn for now. If not, you'll have to wait until we make more."

The people behind me grumbled in anger, and I sighed. "Fine, I'll buy just one bag."

I barely let out a thank you after paying and receiving the paper bag of buttered popcorn, frustrated by the shitty service and scenario. As I walked away, I quickly tried to eat my share of the popcorn before I was going to have to split the bag with Ethan. I could already imagine our butter-covered hands touching in the same bag... I shivered at the uncomfortable thought.

Just as I was about to head toward the stands, though, my eyes fell upon a familiar, tall girl. She was standing next to a garbage bin, talking to someone on her cell phone. Just by the green-streaked hair, I recognized my old friend instantly, who I hadn't talked to in over a year since she had decided to visit her uncle and aunt in Paris.

Ivy Blackthorn was now finally back in town.

As I was about to go up to her, though, I heard her whisper, "*No,* you can't tell her. Can you honestly believe that she won't go crying to the police after hearing what we've done?" Ivy twisted a lock of her long hair nervously.

What the hell is going on?

Intrigued but not wanting to look like a stalker, I ducked and hid behind a nearby tree where I could only hear her voice.

"Look, it's over, okay? She won't be saying anything anymore." There was a pause. "Yes, and I have proof. She's *gone.*" Another pause. "Yes, *Annabeth is dead.*"

The words made me back away from the tree slowly, scared by what I had just heard.

How did she find out? I began to wonder. *Didn't she just get back from Paris? How does Ivy know that Annabeth is dead?*

My head swirled with questions, only increasing my headache. However, as I glanced over at Ethan, who was still sitting on the bleachers, I at least knew one answer.

I knew that I kept protecting myself from reality – from my *real* feelings – and I had to accept the truth. I had to accept that I had killed Annabeth, even if I didn't want to believe it, and I had to accept that Ethan wasn't *just* her brother.

I wanted us to be more than *just friends.*

After all, as complicated as it was, he was everything I ever wanted.

He was that guy that could make me smile on my worst days, only needing to do something stupid to make me laugh.

He was that guy that would tease me about my every bad skill, even though he wasn't any better.

He was that guy that made me want to live – who made me feel alive most.

He was that guy that I was always going to love, no matter what happened.

And that *really* scared me.

Chapter 8
Jessi
Chasing the Devil's Tail

I knew two things for sure.

One, Annabeth Landers was dead, and no one – so it seemed – had gotten closer to figuring out who had killed her.

And two, Ivy Blackthorn was now a suspect.

While I didn't have a ton of evidence to back up my claim, it was a start. I wasn't sure how I felt about knowing a suspect as closely as I did – Ivy and I were *far* from *best friends,* but we knew each other decently well.

What if she finds out that I'm on her tail? I wondered anxiously. *Will I be next? Will she come after me in the middle of the night, during a sleepover–*

I shook my head, focusing on the road in front of me. I would do whatever it took to bring Anna's killer to light. I didn't know where Ivy was now, but I knew that I would find her eventually. Ivy always seemed to show up to ruin my peace at one moment or another.

In the meantime, though, I decided to get the dreaded deed over with.

Talking to Drake.

I knew where Drake lived – unfortunately – since Annabeth had dragged me along more than a fair share of times to "go say hi." However, that had always just been a subtle way of saying "going over for a half an hour conversation and make-out session, while Jessi stands awkwardly to the side." Either I stood there, or I talked to one of his siblings, though they weren't ones for conversation.

Basically, that house was a living embodiment of my nightmares.

Was that why I did what I did? I blinked hard, trying to banish the thought. *It doesn't matter anymore. No one knows.*

Parking my bike on the edge of Drake's driveway, I reluctantly made my way up to his duplex house, trying to make myself look something other than miserable. Once I erased the scowl from my face, I reached up and rang the doorbell. I then backed away and stood on the porch, waiting, the scorching summer sun beating down on my head.

Suddenly, the door swung open, and an imposing girl looked down at me – Leah, Drake's older sister. Her skin was a dark, chestnut brown, as were her eyes, which were rimmed with gold eyeliner. Her jet-black hair was tied back in rows of tiny braids.

"Yes?" she asked, eyeing me with a funny look on her face.

"Is–" I cleared my throat. "Is Drake here?"

Leah kept the funny look on her face, raising an eyebrow. "Why?" she asked suspiciously.

"I'm... I was..." I was still getting used to talking about Anna in the past tense. I took a breath. "I was Annabeth's friend."

Leah leaned against the doorframe, crossing her arms over her chest like she was waiting for more information.

"Jessi?" I said tentatively. When that didn't change her expression, I knew it was time to admit defeat. "The third-wheeler?"

"Sorry, but you just missed him," she declared, twirling one of her braids between her fingers. "He left to go to GV with some friends."

I tried hard not to sigh in exasperation. I knew where the Greenville Conservation and Recreation Area – more commonly known as "GV" – was, but it was twenty-five minutes away by bike. I had biked to GV from my house in the past and had never minded, but twenty-five minutes of biking just to find *Drake* sounded like *way* too much work.

But I had to.

For Anna.

Despite the long bike ride that it required, GV had always been one of my favorite places to be. Many trails sprawled for miles, and there were clear, cool lakes that were the best places to hang out on scorching summer afternoons.

My absolute favorite thing about the area was the trees, though. There were plenty of thick-boughed, low-branched oak trees, and I loved to climb them. Maybe it was a little strange for someone like me to enjoy climbing trees, but I really did. Up there, alone with only the wind and the leaves, I felt free. It was silly and childish, but it almost made me feel like I had wings.

I locked my bike to the rack, then headed over to the huge map near the entrance to GV. I knew quite a few of the trails, but it didn't hurt to double-check.

I had a feeling that I knew where Drake would be since there was a cave near one of the trails, and for some reason, all the boys *loved* to dare each other to go inside. I assumed that they thought a bear was living there, but that was highly unlikely.

The cave was only about ten minutes away – if you knew the right trail to take – so that was a relief. I had already worked *more* than hard enough to track down Drake.

I headed into the forest, following the orange markers that were spray-painted onto the trunks of some of the trees. I glanced around, taking in the dense greenery and patterns of sunlight against the gravel, then came across a small, wooden bridge overlooking the most turbulent portion of a river. The bridge itself was small – not more than ten feet across – and was built with a strange mix of wood. Half of it was dark – an unnaturally dark tone that I had never seen in nature – and half of it was light – maybe birch. A lot of the bridge was now metal since the wood was old and rickety, but the fact that it had been built with such a strange color scheme was interesting.

There was a small, wooden sign in front of the bridge, reading "Ember's Bridge," along with a panel below it that talked about its history. However, I found it quite useless since *everyone* knew the story of Ember Falls.

It had been drilled into our brains since third grade that some colonist had shown up here with his wife, and out of *love,* he had named the town after her. He had also built her a weirdly colored bridge right above the most dangerous part of the river.

How romantic.

When I reached the middle of the bridge, I looked down at the water – where two opposite-facing rapids slammed against each other with undying force. Suddenly, felt a rush as if I had drunk a dozen cups of coffee.

I was used to the feeling by now, though, since it happened every time that I crossed that bridge. It was just nerves, I was sure – looking at those angry rapids while standing on a God-knew-how-old bridge would make anyone nervous.

Stepping off the bridge, I shook out my limbs, ridding myself of the last of the strange jittery energy. After walking for a few more minutes, I finally started to hear the adrenaline-drunk laughter of teenage boys from nearby. I slowed down my brisk pace and tried to steady my breathing. I had to seem calm and composed. After all, a bunch of seventeen and eighteen-year-old boys wouldn't give answers to a stressed-out, fidgety seventeen-year-old girl.

Once I made sure that I was put together, I headed up the small hill that led to the cave. As expected, about a dozen teenage boys were spending time together nearby. Some of them were perched up in trees, and some of them were sitting with their legs dangling over the entrance of the cave.

"Hello?" I spoke, though no one acknowledged me. I cleared my throat and repeated more loudly, "*Hello?*" A few heads turned my way, surveying me with bored expressions. "I'm looking for Drake Rachford. Know where he is?"

One boy hopped down from his perch above the overhang, landing heavily on the gravel pathway. Once he stood up, I got a better look at him and nearly smiled. The boy had dark-toned skin, brown eyes, and deep brown hair that had fallen into his eyes, which he quickly combed out of his face. "I hear you're looking for me?" he asked, raising an eyebrow.

I rolled my eyes at Drake's attempt at mysteriousness. "Congratulations, Sherlock."

Drake rolled his eyes back at me. "What do you want?"

I gestured for him to follow me, ignoring his moronic friends, who made crude jokes from up in the tree. Drake reluctantly followed me down the path, though before he could speak again, I jumped in. "I want to talk about Annabeth." I made sure that my voice was steady and hard with no signs of weakness.

Drake looked appalled. "Annabeth?"

"Yes. Start talking."

Drake combed his dark hair out of his face, and I tried hard not to roll my eyes. "Annabeth," he said slowly, then took a long pause as if saying the name exhausted him. "Why?"

I crossed my arms in frustration. "I was her friend — her *best friend*. I want to know how other people remember her. And, if you could give me other references, that would be great."

"Listen, Jessica—"

"Jessi," I corrected, anger boiling inside of me. "Just *Jessi*. Not *Jessica*. My name is *Jessi.* No correlation with Jessica."

"Jessi," he repeated. "I don't exactly feel like talking about—"

I stopped walking and turned on my heel, glaring at him. "I don't care if you want to talk or not. This is important."

Drake glared back. "Why do *I* have to say anything? You have no authority over me. I could just walk away right now."

"But you won't because Annabeth mattered to you as much as she did to me." That was a *bit* of a stretch and very sappy, but when Drake's expression faltered, I realized that this method was working.

"She was great," he started, as I began to smile in triumph. "Dependable, you know? Sporty, too. She knew all the rules to all the sports, so I never had to waste time explaining them to her." Drake had a faraway look in his brown eyes. "Great girl, overall. And as far as other people go, I can't say I have anyone else in mind. Besides you and that Adley girl, Anna didn't seem to have any close friends."

I looked at the ground so that Drake wouldn't be able to see the dark glare I knew my features had twisted into.

This whole trip was for nothing.

"It's fine, thanks anyway," I told him before Drake cast me a smile and turned around, sprinting back toward his group of friends. "It's fine," I whispered to the trees. A small gray squirrel cocked its head at me, then ran off. "It's fine."

But it *wasn't* fine.

I had only a single lead, and even that was shaky.

"It's fine."

I needed to cool off. I was seriously glad that I wasn't inside a building because I knew that if I *had* been, the room would've felt as if it was closing in on me.

Sitting high up in a tree, I breathed in a lungful of warm summer air, watching a few ducks bob in and out of the lake below. I then closed my eyes, trying to forget about the confrontation I'd just had with Drake.

"One for tree-climbing too, Short Stack? Does it make you feel tall?"

I turned my head toward the annoyingly familiar voice that had interrupted my thoughts. "So it seems."

Ivy pulled herself up onto a branch beside mine, flashing her trademark smirk. "I'll always be taller."

I glared at Ivy. "Why do you keep *talking* to me? Why are you still acknowledging me after an entire year of being gone? I'm honestly surprised your minuscule brain *still* remembers me."

"I'm wounded, Short Stack," Ivy remarked with a frown, though I could tell that she was putting on an act. "I remember you and your whole gang of weirdos. Adley, Ethan, Annabeth–" She cut herself off, suddenly looking uneasy.

Aha, I thought. *Time to get her talking.*

Of course, I didn't know what I would do if she *was* Annabeth's killer.

Should I run, or would she catch me? Would I be her next victim? I shook my head, trying to clear my thoughts. I needed to focus.

"Annabeth," I repeated. "Surely by now, you know that she's dead." I wasn't sure how I was keeping my voice so calm – just saying those words made me want to scream.

Ivy looked around hastily as if she wanted to find the nearest escape route. "Everyone knows," she said, still not meeting my eyes. "Stuff goes around fast in a small town. News, gossip, diseases."

I leaned forward on my branch. "Yes, it does, but you knew Annabeth *personally*. And so did I." Ivy met my eyes, and her jade-green ones were bright with alarm. "So, can we talk this out? Annabeth's-friend-to-Annabeth's-friend?"

"Listen, I didn't know your little girlfriend as well as you did–"

"Quit avoiding the subject!" I shouted so loudly that a few House sparrows flew away from a nearby tree. "Just talk. Tell me what you know." I softened my tone, hoping that a nicer approach would work on her. "I want to know how everyone remembers her." I couldn't believe that I was still sticking with the memoir lie, but it seemed to have been working.

"She was Annabeth. There's not much else to say." Ivy fidgeted with one of her black fingerless gloves. "Ember Falls' shining little star. Such a *perfect* little angel." Ivy was starting to rant, a dark look suddenly crossing her face. I held my breath, knowing that this could be the turning point of my investigation. "*Too* perfect. I knew that she wouldn't ever keep her mouth shut–" Ivy suddenly stopped speaking, her olive-toned skin paling a shade. "Shit," she whispered under her breath.

She knew that she had said too much.

Suddenly, Ivy glanced down at her phone. "I, uh, have to go. See you around." Then, Ivy swung off her branch, landing underneath me with a hard smack against the gravel before walking down another path.

I wanted to say something – scream at her, really – but I suddenly felt frozen. Ivy's words kept echoing in my head.

I knew that she wouldn't ever keep her mouth shut.

If Ivy was worried about Anna reporting her, she would have wanted to keep Anna's mouth shut. *Permanently.*

I started to tremble uncontrollably.

Ivy had a motive to kill.

Chapter 9
Adley
A Demon Disguised as an Angel

The warm breeze blew through my curls as I arrived in front of Ember Falls High, nerves knotting in my stomach. Though the burgundy-bricked building wasn't large and intimidating as city schools looked, the teenagers were the size of skyscrapers.

I definitely wasn't in middle school anymore.

I tried to focus on the warm and welcoming grounds, which were decorated with welcoming banners and signs announcing the annual First of October Bonfire. After entering, I glanced around, trying to see if I recognized anyone from my old school. I walked up the staircase, in search of my new locker, as voices buzzed with excitement, teenagers chatting and hugging one another all around.

"A!" I heard a familiar voice squeal from behind, and I turned to see my best friend sprinting toward me. She then wrapped me in her arms, squeezing me to death. "Welcome to high school, bitch!"

Annabeth had her long, loose, blonde curls falling over her shoulders, as usual, and she was wearing a white-and-yellow floral-printed black dress. She had also accessorized with a black belt that wrapped around her impossibly tiny waist and had thrown on a pair of black platform heels that were decorated with white rhinestones. She even had a glowing tan, unlike me, who was as pale as the dead from staying cooped up all summer long indoors.

"Hey, how was volleyball camp?" I asked her as excitement bubbled in my chest. We hadn't seen each other in two months – it had been the longest that we had ever been separated.

"It was amazing – I met so many cool people and have finally mastered my spikes. Though I've heard that the competition is tough, I'm going to nail tryouts this year."

"You were the Queen of Serves in middle school – I'm sure you'll impress everyone here too."

"I guess we'll see." Anna shrugged, then glanced over her shoulder at the black, rusted lockers behind us. "Are these ours?"

I glanced down at my schedule to confirm, then nodded and opened my locker. I tossed a couple of textbooks inside, and Anna did the same before we started to walk toward our first-period class.

Just as we were rounding a corner, though, a short brunette ran into me, dropping her books onto my feet. She started to apologize non-stop as she gathered her books and stood back up.

"Watch it next time, freak. These shoes are vintage," I retorted, rubbing my black knee-high boots to see if the girl *had managed to scratch them – lucky for her, she hadn't.*

Once she was standing, though, her large brown eyes suddenly widened. "Annabeth!" she cried, her voice filled with joy as she stared at my best friend.

The odd girl with warm brown skin had her chin-length bob of cocoa-brown hair messy and loose, and she was so short that her head was beside my shoulders. For a moment, I thought she was a seventh grader from the middle of nowhere – her outfit definitely screamed it. After all, she looked like she had just rolled out of a haystack in a farmhouse and had thrown on a pair of farmers' overalls on top of a black t-shirt covered in white lint.

"Hey," Anna replied enthusiastically, and when I realized that she actually meant it – unlike she normally did when she was polite to strangers – I snapped my head in her direction, baffled. Anna tried hugging the odd-looking child, though it looked so awkward with the five-inch height difference. It was almost embarrassing to watch.

I wore a look of disgust on my face as the basketcase grinned. However, Anna then caught my glare and rolled her eyes at me. My jaw almost dropped.

What has gotten *into* her? *I thought, staring at the two girls in astonishment. I knew that Anna had always tried to be nice to everybody, but it was impossible not to react the way that I did when staring at the odd bird.* What is Anna seeing?

"Adley, this is my friend from volleyball camp, Jessi," Anna explained as the weird girl waved at me. She was attempting to look up at me, but since I was much taller, I caught her staring at my boobs for a second.

"Um, up here," I snapped, and the bizarre girl's cheeks flushed pink before I looked over at Anna. "Your friend?" I questioned as I looked the creep up and down from out of the corner of my eye. The Anna that I had known would never have become friends with an outsider – she would have only been polite to them. But Anna nodded, so I tried to be nice. "Hi," I said to the outcast, trying to not sound like I was talking to a four-year-old – I was sure that it had come out sounding that way.

"Hi," the whack job replied enthusiastically. "I am such a fan of Guns and Roses."

I stared at her, confused until she pointed to the black t-shirt that I was wearing, which had two silver guns and red roses all over it, the band name written across in white writing. It was tucked into my pair of denim shorts. "Oh, you mean the band?" I asked the strange girl.

"Yeah. Aren't you considered a fan if you wear their merchandise?"

I laughed. "Oh, I guess. Though I just thought that it looked cute!" I looked over at Anna, expecting a witty comment, but all she did was stand quietly.

What has gotten *into* her–?

"Welcome back, Ember Falls' Eagles," announced a familiar voice over the PA system, which I recognized as Marissa Langford, the head of the volleyball team.

The blaring noise shook me back to reality, where I realized that I was leaning against my old, rusted locker from three years before – without Anna by my side.

"In all seriousness, I want to start the year by

informing you that we lost a very special student a few weeks ago." When Marissa started sniffling, I froze, knowing exactly what was going to follow. *"Annabeth Landers will always be in our hearts. She was a shining star on the volleyball court and will forever be with us. That's why the volleyball squad has decided to create a GoFundMe page to support her – her murderer will be brought to justice."* After a moment of silence, Marissa then cheered, *"Now, go Eagles!"*

The warning bell sounded once the PA system shut off, but I didn't move, a hot tear running down my face. Were they fucking *serious* – a *GoFundMe page*? Anna would have hated that – yet somehow, that was the only thing this school was willing to do to honor her.

A fucking *donation* website.

I rubbed the tear away harshly with the back of my hand.

I guessed nobody had ever known the real Anna – not like I had.

Looking up from my tray, which held a plate of the first day of school's spaghetti and meatballs, I walked over to the picnic tables where Anna was waiting for me. Sitting down across from her at a black metal table, I sat my white polka-dotted black bag beside me and took a forkful of my pasta just as she did. I then swallowed it fast before taking a huge gulp of water from my metal water bottle since the pasta tasted like something that could be found in a dumpster.

"God, remind me to start bringing a lunch," Anna laughed, as she began to search through her neon pink school bag to find a snack. "I swear, I always thought that

high school lunches were supposed to taste better than the ones in middle school."

"Yeah, same," I agreed as I dug through my school bag's pockets, hoping to find a snack – but I didn't. "Hey, would you rather eat that pasta for lunch or eat broken glass for dessert?"

Anna looked up from her bag and threw on a thinking face – I could tell that she was holding back a laugh. "I think I might take my chances with the poisonous pasta."

"Oh, I don't know. That broken glass sounds tempting," I giggled as Anna bit into the chocolate chip cookie that she had found wrapped in her bag.

"Ooh, my turn..." She trailed off as her sapphire-blue eyes searched the now-crowded picnic table area until she spotted a group of boys hanging out in the parking lot. I could tell that she was specifically staring at the tall boy with sandy blond hair, who was wearing a brown leather jacket – his signature item. "Would you rather date Nate Tucker *or–" she stopped herself as she gazed around the school grounds until her eyes glued to a boy sitting alone underneath a nearby tree, reading* The Outsiders. *"...Ethan?"*

"You bitch!" *I screamed teasingly. "You just want me to admit how I feel about a guy that I barely know."*

"You don't *barely know him – we've been going to school with him since first grade," Anna reminded me before watching me intently as if waiting for an answer.*

"Fine, Nate."

"Finally – it's been too obvious. Do you know how long I've been trying to make you say it out loud?"

"Yes, since middle school grad," I said, exasperated.

"You know I hate admitting these things."

"But I know *you'd* never confess to having a crush on my brother, of all people, just to save yourself."

"Ha-ha." I rolled my eyes, then narrowed them as I spotted the familiar short brunette from this morning bounce toward us. I tapped Anna's shoulder and brought her attention toward the intruder. "Oh, look who it is. Seems like you have a secret admirer," I purred, and Anna slapped my arm, shutting me up.

"Hey!" Jessi squeaked in her annoying voice. Somehow, she looked even worse in the broad daylight, which highlighted this big, ugly bruise that circled over her right eye.

"What's up, Dalmatian? Did you lose your pack?" I snickered.

"You're such a bitch," Anna snapped, and my eyes widened in shock — she actually meant it.

"Sorry, I was only joking." I flashed the outcast a fake smile before tapping my hand on the bench next to me at the table. "Come sit with us, Jessica."

She ignored my offer and took a seat next to Anna, not seeming to notice how I had purposely screwed up her name.

It was then silent as if a cloud of awkwardness had rolled in, shadowing the table. Absentmindedly, my eyes wandered around the schoolyard until they stopped on the student parking lot again.

"What are you looking at?" I heard the weirdo question, though I didn't care to reply.

"Darling, it's not what she's looking at — it's who."

"Who?" I heard the freak ask Anna, though it sounded as if she was questioning the word itself.

Anna decided to answer the opposite definition. "Adley's new boyfriend, Nathaniel Tuck–"

"Shut up!" I cut her off, feeling my face burn with embarrassment. "Nate isn't my boyfriend. He doesn't even know me."

The wide-eyed owl seemed puzzled, her eyebrows furrowing. "Why not?"

"I don't think you know who he is," Anna began. "He's one of the popular guys in our grade – he was back in middle school and still looks like it today."

"So, why would he know us?" I finished.

The odd duck still looked confused but stayed quiet for a moment, probably not wanting to argue. "If he doesn't already know you, why don't you just introduce yourself to him? You know, go over and talk to him?"

Anna and I laughed as if it was the funniest joke that we had ever heard.

"Talk to him? No, you wait for him to make the first move," Anna explained matter-of-factly.

The tree stump's shoulders slumped, her face falling. "What-what do you mean? Why can't you make the first move?"

"Because then I'd look desperate," I thought aloud, laughing.

"You have so much to learn, Little J." Anna then shushed us to grab our attention. "Oh, look, he's coming!"

Anna and I got into character and started laughing, trying to grab Nate's attention subtly. Little J tried to join us *but didn't play the part so well – she was terrible at acting.*

"Hey," Nate called when he passed our table, carrying a basketball under one of his muscular arms as his two friends followed behind him. He flashed us a wide, bright smile, and I almost fainted.

"Hey," I replied before Anna could as my heart thumped rapidly in its ribcage.

"I can't believe it's you, after all this time."

"I know," I sighed until the words hit me, and I was struck out of my daze. "Wait, *what*?"

"Are you okay? You don't look okay…"

I blinked hard, convinced that I was still dreaming. I didn't believe it at first, but once I noticed that I was alone, standing in front of a picnic table without Anna or Jessi, I dropped my tray, which the table luckily caught.

Because right in front of me still stood Nate Tucker.

"Nate?" I questioned, baffled as he cut through the school grounds to stand next to me.

But how?

"Yeah, it's me. My family and I just moved back into town yesterday. Turns out, my dad was relocated here, so we're moving back." He pulled me into a hug, whispering, "I'm really happy that we'll get to spend our last year here together." After pulling back, he added, "I'm gonna go get lunch, but when I come back, you can update me on *everything*."

Before I had a chance to say anything, Nate walked off. His wide, bright smile was back on his face as he entered the school through the side door.

What just happened?

"He's *back*?" Jessi asked in what sounded like disgust. I spun around to see her taking a seat at the table in front of me. She nudged over my polka-dotted school bag, which now wasn't so new, with multiple tiny holes lining the fabric.

I chuckled, thinking back to how Nate now looked. His hazel eyes were still the same, as well as his perfectly tanned skin, though his wavy hair was a darker shade of sandy blond.

"Hello?" Jessi waved a hand as if she wanted to try to get my attention. I looked down at her, then decided to sit, as much as I wanted to leave. "So, are you guys back together or something?"

"I-I don't know." The question took me by surprise – I thought we had broken up years ago. "We've barely talked. He said that he'd be right back, and then, I could tell him everything... I don't know what's gonna happen to us."

That butterfly-fluttering feeling came back into my stomach, making me feel nauseous. After what had happened a week ago with Ethan – who I hadn't spoken to since – I hadn't even wanted to think about relationships.

Of course, having Nate back changed things.

"Distract me, okay? How has your first day been going?"

"I'm popular!" Jessi cried, and I had to put in a huge amount of effort not to roll my eyes.

"*Popular?* No offense, Jess, but do you even *know* the definition of popularity?"

"Shut up, A!" she snapped. "Some kid overheard my

conversation with Ivy Blackthorn last Monday at GV and sent a hint to the writer of TheTea.com!"

"*What?* You, of all people, were talking to *Ivy Blackthorn?*" I asked Jessi, somehow feeling a little jealous that she had gotten to talk to my old friend before I had even gotten to. "Why?"

"Because Anna had *apparently* hung around Ivy a few times – Ethan told me so."

"Aha! You *were* talking to Ethan just to get new leads for your investigation. I knew it couldn't have been for some stupid *memoir of sorts,*" I remarked, overly excited about being right.

"How did you know about that?"

"Ethan told *me* about it after I hung out with him last week."

"You guys *hung out?*" Jessi's oversized eyes looked as if they were going to pop out of her skull. "I thought he was just *Anna's brother.*"

I was quiet for a second, contemplating if I should reply or not until I remembered something. "Wait, Anna and Ivy had *hung out?*" The idea only struck me then, confusing me. I knew that Anna had known Ivy – obviously since I used to talk with her – but *personally?* It just sounded bizarre.

"Yeah, where have you been for the last minute? Ethan *literally* told me that they used to talk. Plus, after talking to Drake" –she made a gagging face– "who made me bike to GV and didn't help at all, I ran into Ivy, who I had known would be the next best lead. And she was."

That was when Jessi took out her BlackBerry and pulled up the site to TheTea.com, the most popular gossip blog in Ember Falls. She showed me the post with a picture of her and Ivy in an oak tree at GV. Underneath was written the conversation that they'd had together that day, from the first hi to Ivy's suspicious goodbye.

"And that was the *exact* conversation," Jessi stated with a smirk. I was surprised that she wasn't finding that freaky at all.

"Ivy had said that Anna couldn't keep her mouth shut? About what?" I asked as I leaned my elbows against the table. I couldn't help but be intrigued.

"I don't know. She never told me."

"Wait, I *may* know why," I exclaimed, then quickly recapped the day at the park with Ethan, sharing Ivy's conversation that I had overheard. I sometimes stretched out the truth *just* a little, but how could I not? Ivy *was* my old friend, but then again, I needed to be off the radar.

Sometimes, you had to think of yourself before others.

Besides, who said that Ivy didn't deserve to get in trouble? Somehow, she had still been managing to stay low and not get caught for every criminal act she had committed years before. However, she couldn't help looking guilty for doing something involving Anna.

All I had to do was make the facts official, and Ivy's record wouldn't have been close to clean anymore.

I grabbed Jessi's phone from her hands and started typing an email to the address belonging to TheTea.com.

"What are you *doing*?" she hissed, trying to take her phone back as I held it high in the air.

"Sending a hint on what we know about Ivy and the

night of Anna's murder so that it can go public. I mean, it *is* Ivy who murdered Anna, right?"

"*Maybe*, but by making the intel public, it'll give Ivy a chance to run."

I immediately stopped typing and dropped my arms to my sides.

Jessi was *right*.

"Don't worry. I've got a plan. Ivy will pay for the crime that she committed *no matter what*." Normally, Jessi's determination would have annoyed me, but now, I only felt happier.

Without anything else to say, and too overjoyed to risk ruining the fact that I was off the hook, I got up from my spot. I threw my school bag strap over my shoulder, then dropped Jessi's phone back onto the table. I picked up my tray, throwing the untouched lunch into the nearby trashcan before leaving.

"Where are you going? Aren't you going to wait for Nate?"

"If he comes back, tell him I had to get to class early," I told Jessi, and for once, she didn't ask any questions.

"So sorry about back there at lunch – and this morning at the lockers," Anna remarked, smiling as she placed down her books on the desk beside mine in the empty, dark classroom. I hadn't wanted to be late for any of my classes on my first day of high school, so I decided to arrive early for math after lunch.

"It's fine. I'm just confused about why you would want to talk to that odd bird."

"She does look like a bird, doesn't she?" Anna laughed, sounding like her usual self again as she sat down in her chair. She then sighed, twirling a strand of hair. "Look, I'm doing this for our dads. Yes, Jessi and I met at camp, but when our dads bumped into each other the other day at Speedway, they reconnected – apparently, they went to school together back in the day."

"So, you're being nice to her for the sake of your dad?"

"Exactly – I can't just go around being a bitch to her. Our fathers are happy that we are friends, and it would be awkward if we suddenly weren't." As I nodded, Anna added with a smile, "As I've taught you, to have people love you – as obnoxious as they may be – you must make them believe that you love them too. Fake it until you make it – or in this case, just fake it."

I laughed, relieved that Anna hadn't yet lost her mind. "Sorry, I didn't get the hint. I can pretend with you from now on, though. I promise."

Anna sighed, twirling a strand of her wavy hair with a finger covered in gold rings. "You don't pretend, A – you become the lie itself. Take my reputation – I had to create an entirely new persona to make everyone believe that I'm some angel from Heaven so that I would be liked." She laughed softly. "But now, aren't I always the favorite?"

The warning bell rang, shaking me from my daze at my desk in chemistry class. Thinking back, I had known that Anna had been *very* secretive – I had been the only one that she would tell everything to.

Well, that was what I had *thought.* But was there a possibility that she had been hiding other things from me, like hanging out with Ivy?

Nobody could ever tell what Anna was hiding behind that angel-like face of hers since she had everybody fooled. She had built herself a shining-star reputation, and it was who everyone thought the *real* Annabeth Landers was. I had been the only person in the entire world who had known how bad she had *really* been.

She'd had her boyfriends, her friends, her parents, and even her brother under a spell.

That was how good of a liar my best friend was.

Chapter 10

Jessi

Gossip Travels Fast in Ember Falls

It was only lunchtime, and things were already getting weird.

For starters, Adley's ex-boyfriend was back in town, and Adley wasn't taking it so well.

And secondly, I was now a star on TheTea.com, Ember Falls' notorious gossip blog. I wasn't a huge gossiper, but lately, I had been looking on there for clues since Anna had been quite the gossiper herself. I had luckily found an article that someone had written recently, focusing on me and Ivy. They had meticulously written our whole conversation from GV, down to the last detail.

In other circumstances, I would've found that creepy. But now, I didn't mind it at all. It meant that I wasn't the only one who had found Ivy's demeanor more than a little suspicious.

Ever since Adley had left a couple of minutes ago to head to class early, I had been staring at the article. I had read it a million times, but I couldn't stop looking at it – it just felt too *odd*.

Sure, there were a lot of gossip bloggers out there, eager for anything. But the fact that they had caught the conversation that had revealed that Ivy had something against Anna, who was now *dead...*

It felt like it couldn't have just been a coincidence.

Then again, the "bad girl" and the "good girl" talking was easily more than enough to make any gossiper want to record our conversation.

I shut off my phone and tucked it into the side pocket of my school bag. I then packed up my lunch bag, searching around for something to do besides sitting alone for the next half an hour.

What an amazing *start to the first day of senior year.*

Suddenly, I caught sight of Ethan – who would have usually been playing soccer with his group of friends. He was now sitting alone at a nearby table and staring at a group of guys playing basketball on the gravel in the distance.

He looked, to be quite honest, *miserable.*

Not that I could blame him.

I stood up and slowly made my way over to him, giving him a small wave once he noticed me.

"Hey, Jessi," he greeted, smiling sadly at me.

"Hey," I said, sitting down on the bench beside him. "You okay?"

"Oh, yeah." Ethan absentmindedly glanced toward the main doors that Adley had darted through a few minutes ago. "Just thinking."

"That's dangerous," I teased gently. "What about?"

Ethan sighed as he raked a hand through his messy, blond curls that were so similar to Anna's that it made me flinch. "Many things." He looked again toward the doors.

"Are you waiting for someone?" I asked since all his door-glancing was *seriously* giving him away — the Landers weren't the subtlest of people, to say the least.

"No, not really." Ethan flushed red, then looked back at me. "I just saw Adley running back inside, and I was wondering if she was going to come back out."

"She probably won't, honestly. She's dealing with—"

"Yo, E!" a voice suddenly shouted, and both Ethan and I turned to see three guys coming toward us.

I had met Ethan's friends a couple of times before, and — to be completely honest — they *scared* me. There was Dylan, the loudest and craziest out of them, who had shoulder-length, brown hair, and always wore a plaid sweater and a pair of sweatpants. There was also Kyle, who, as shy as he could be, always had a bone to pick with Dylan. He had messy dark hair and bright blue eyes, and he dressed more traditionally with a pair of jeans and a buttoned shirt. Lastly, there was Calvin, who was the peacemaker and logical one in the group. He had black hair and always stuck to wearing blue jeans and a plain-colored shirt, along with his baseball cap.

"Have you *seen* who's back?" Dylan cried, sliding into the spot next to Ethan as Kyle and Calvin sat across from me. Dylan fixed his gray beanie so that it concealed most of his messy hair.

Ethan shook his head. "No...?"

"So, wait." Kyle looked at Ethan, combing a hand

through the black-brown hair that had fallen into his eyes. "You haven't seen him yet?"

"Well, we *all* know how oblivious Ethan can be," Dylan proclaimed, elbowing Ethan lightly.

"What are you *talking* about?" Ethan sighed.

"Nate Tucker's back," Dylan blurted, and I couldn't tell if he was excited about this or not.

"What?" Ethan sputtered, paling. "Really?"

Calvin nodded, rolling his eyes. "As unfortunate as it is, he *is* back. And it won't be long before he starts torturing everyone again."

"It's not *fair*," Dylan whined, rapidly shifting from excited to sad. "I just *know* that he's gonna steal my spot as soccer team captain this year."

"*That's* your biggest issue?" Kyle hissed, narrowing his blue eyes at Dylan.

"Well, *duh*! It's *senior year–*"

"Can you two quit it?" Calvin complained, then looked over at Ethan. "You good over there?"

"I-I'm fine," Ethan stuttered, but he didn't look okay. He was breathing deeply, and he was clearly zoning out every few seconds. "I'm just shocked, I guess."

"It must really suck for you since he used to be Adley's boyfriend," Dylan mused, then yelped as Kyle punched him in the arm.

Ethan's face went bright red, and I facepalmed, feeling embarrassed *for* him.

After years of awkward stares, comments, and blushed cheeks, I finally realized that Ethan had a crush on Adley. I wasn't sure if she liked him back, though, which was why I had been so surprised to hear that the two of them had spent time together the other day.

"*And* I think it's time for us to go," Calvin said, standing up. "See you later in class, E?"

Ethan nodded, looking dazedly at the guys as they walked off.

"So," I stated, trying to fill the awkward silence, "that just happened."

Ethan shook his head, then looked back at me, obviously done with the conversation. "Are you gonna try out for volleyball this year, Jess?"

I blinked hard. Just the word "volleyball" sent a jolt through me as if I had been electrocuted. "I haven't thought about it," I lied – all I had thought about the night before was volleyball, and whether I should try out or not since it felt *wrong* without Anna there.

"I think Anna would have wanted you to," Ethan remarked softly as if he had been reading my thoughts.

"I don't know. I'll see," I told him, unsure if I was ready to face volleyball without Anna.

But could I do it *for* her?

After school was insanely busy as always – cars honking; parents trying to pick up their kids; teenagers driving recklessly in their new cars. I was too distracted to care, though. My mind was racing as I thought about the stupid thing that I had just done.

Writing my name on the volleyball sign-up sheet.

My bus usually arrived later than most, so I liked to sit under the shade of the nearby tree and read. But as I approached my spot, I noticed that this time, another person occupied it.

"All right, but hurry up! I've been waiting out here for *ten minutes.*" I found Adley standing under the tree, her cell phone pressed to her ear. She mumbled something, sighed into the receiver a final time, then hung up.

"What are you doing here?" I asked Adley after wandering over to where she stood.

Adley rolled her eyes. "Ethan's running behind since a teacher wanted to see him after class."

"I see," I mumbled, looking down at my sneakers. "Hard day?"

Adley's eyes suddenly narrowed, and I realized that I had definitely said the wrong thing. "What do you think?" she sneered, and before I could say anything more, she added, "You think this is funny, don't you? I know you've always hated Nate."

"*What?*"

"God, you'd *never* understand." Adley glared at me like my very presence was making her angry. "I should be talking to *Anna. She* would understand me."

Of course, *Adley* of all people would bring up Annabeth for selfish reasons.

"*That's* the only reason you're sad that Annabeth is *gone*? Because you can't talk to her about *boys* anymore," I snapped, adding fuel to the fire that Adley had started.

"Well, who *else* would I want to talk to?" Adley retorted, cheeks flushing a furious red. "*You* don't know anything about relationships."

We had begun to attract a crowd with our raised voices, and everyone in it looked as if they were anticipating a fight. I felt angry enough to give them one.

"Maybe I don't know anything because I never had the *chance*!"

Oh, God, what the hell did I just say?

Adley stepped back, raising an eyebrow in confusion. I didn't give her the chance to say anything. "Forget it. It's *pointless* arguing with you," I mumbled before shoving past the crowd around us and walking in the direction of my street.

"Where are you going?" Adley cried, frustration lacing her voice.

I didn't say anything back. I didn't feel like I could with the laughter and shouts of people following, and especially the concerned voice belonging to Ethan as he asked Adley what was going on.

Tears burning my eyes, I ran down the sidewalk, away from the school, away from the prying eyes, away from Adley.

Away from Annabeth's past.

Though I wasn't sure if I would ever be able to escape that.

Chapter 11
Adley
The Hauntings from Beneath the Grave

The second day of junior year was the first time that I had been forced to look into Ethan's eyes after the baseball game. We had talked on the way home from school the day before, but it hadn't been the same.

It had just felt *awkward.*

And, of course, it was inevitable that we'd run into each other again, this time diving for the last window seat available in math class during first period. Somehow, the desk was still available, though it was the best seat out of every spot in the classroom. It had great lighting, it gave a spectacular view of the school grounds, and it was the best spot to lose yourself.

I pounced on it first, throwing myself onto the tiny desk as if it was my prey. I didn't even realize that it was Ethan who I was competing against until I saw him roll his eyes from the corner of my own.

He took the last available seat, which was next to me.

"Every year?" he questioned, laughing to himself.

"Of course," I remarked, flashing him an innocent smile as I sat down.

The last bell then rang, and the teacher began the lesson. I took out my books and started to daze out like I usually did, which was probably the reason why I was never the top student in my classes. Usually, I liked to ponder. But this time, every racing thought intensified my pounding headache.

For starters, I couldn't stop thinking about my fight with Jessi after school the day before. Why had she been so *snappy*?

Maybe I don't know anything because I never had the chance*!*

What was *that* supposed to mean? Jessi was seventeen – she had plenty more time to have a relationship. Why complain, saying that she never got the chance? And why be mad at *me,* out of all people? I had done *nothing* to deserve such bullshit from her.

And the other – most obvious – thought was about Nate. After the way we had ended things two years ago, I believed that I was *never* going to hear from him again. Ethan had been the guy that I was going to choose, but now, here was Nate, acting as if two years hadn't passed.

As if he hadn't broken my heart into a trillion little pieces before leaving for New York.

Unless, for him, breaking up because of not wanting to do long-distance meant that we *hadn't* broken up?

No matter what, I still didn't know how I felt about him. I wished that I didn't have to decide instantly

– I wanted *time*.

"*Adley*, what is the solution for 'x' that'll make the statement $2^x=32$ true?"

Waking me from my daze, I looked ahead and away from the window to notice Ms. Peters staring at me with her scary, bright green eyes. She was waiting for an answer to the problem that I hadn't yet solved.

Who needs to find x when I have my own to deal with?

"Um, 'x' must equal 5?" I guessed, which had seemed like a good enough answer in my head.

"Correct," the teacher beamed, suddenly looking pleased with herself. As she turned her gaze toward the rest of the class, I sank into my chair, filled with relief.

Ethan chuckled, his purple-striped pencil still moving extremely fast across his lined notebook page. I didn't understand how he was able to pay attention for so long in this class – why he *cared* that much.

I knew that senior year mattered most, though. I needed a good score on the SATs to get into the college of my choice – and I hadn't done so well on my PSATs.

As I was about to pick up my pencil and attempt to write something down – if he was able to, so was I – I heard a notification come in on my phone. It intrigued me to bend down and pull it out of the side pocket of my school bag.

Nate
8:50 AM
Meet me on the steps after school :)

Sighing as the message started up the never-ending thread of thoughts in my head, I told myself that I couldn't start pushing him away. I had Ethan, but after remembering what Nate and I once had, I *had* to give us another shot.

Nate was already sitting on the cement steps of the school's front entrance when I exited the building after school. Teenagers who were about to be late for their buses were hurrying around him. He was easy to spot since he was wearing his signature brown leather jacket and a pair of black jeans.

A knot formed in the pit of my stomach at the sight of him. I threw on a smile, though, as I walked over and sat down beside him.

"I'm really happy you came," he said, hugging me. I wrapped my arms around him to return the embrace as awkward as it felt.

When I backed away and looked into his green-brown eyes, though, all I wanted was to feel like I used to for him. But it was hard when I still didn't know where we stood. "So, what's new with you?" I asked, trying to make conversation as the commotion around us died down and the schoolyard emptied.

"Not much. My dad's back in town now—"

"So I've heard. How was New York City? Was it as fabulous as we had always dreamed? Did you meet anyone new?"

One of the nights back in ninth grade, when we had first started going out, we had stopped for hot fudge sundaes at Dairy Queen. There, we talked all about what we wanted our futures to look like. I had wanted to go to NYU to major in filmmaking, and surprisingly, Nate had wanted to do the same thing.

"It was nice. I had made some friends, but that group of guys could never be compared to the friendships that I had made here," he admitted, and I smiled sadly.

"Did you hook up with any hot celebrities?" I joked.

"Nah, Paris Hilton had *totally* tried flirting with me one night at this bar, but I knew that I could *never* replace you like that," he chuckled, and I could tell that he was playing along.

"I mean, if it had been *Paris Hilton*," I started. I then looked down at the cement steps, thinking of what I should have *really* been asking. "So, you *didn't* date anyone while you were gone?"

"No, of course, not!" he replied, sounding as if the answer was obvious. "I know we had broken up, but that was only because we couldn't be in the same place. I still want *you*, Adley."

His words hit me, smacking the air out of my lungs for a minute – he *wanted* me. All this time, when he could have been hooking up with much hotter girls in New York, he had waited for me.

He had chosen *me*.

"Nate." I grabbed his hands in mine. I didn't know what to say besides one thing. "I-I have to get something off my chest before this conversation can go any further."

"Of course, what is it?" he squeezed my hands. I glanced down at my lap, unable to meet his eyes.

Maybe this was horrible timing since he had just admitted how he still had feelings for me. But I couldn't stand the idea of talking about my future without him knowing that my best friend didn't have one anymore.

"Anna's dead, Nate."

Nate's face fell, and his grip on my hands tightened. "She's *gone*?" he asked shakily, though he looked calmer than I had expected him to act.

"She was murdered two weeks ago."

"Wh-*What*? Why would someone *do* such a thing?"

"I-I don't know," I said softly, hating that I had to lie to him too. Tears formed in my eyes, and my body trembled. "The police are still trying to get answers, but I knew that you deserved to know." I wiped my face with the back of my hands, about to stand up. "Maybe this isn't the best time to talk about our futures–"

I suddenly felt Nate's warm lips on mine. I leaned into him, forgetting about everything we had just talked about.

"I'm sorry, I know that was horrible timing. But I hated the idea of waiting to do that," he whispered as our lips parted and our foreheads touched. "Fuck, I had been thinking about doing that ever since I left you. I don't know if you still feel the same, but–"

Before he could continue rambling, I leaned over again and kissed him back. Feeling his lips on mine made my old feelings for him resurface as if they had never faded. We were suddenly back in ninth grade, soaked in the rain that had drenched us after our sundaes at Dairy Queen and kissing for the first time.

I wanted him more than ever.

"Wow, I guess I haven't missed much," a snarky voice stated from behind, unpausing time and bringing me back to reality.

"I guess not," I replied, licking my lips and laughing as Nate and I got shoved apart by Ivy. She squeezed in between us after throwing her black crossbody purse and heavy textbooks down on the step behind us. She wore her usual black palette-based outfit – Rolling Stones tee, short high-waisted skirt, fishnet tights, and combat boots.

"Welcome back, Natty," Ivy exclaimed as she crossed one of her long legs over the other. "I have to say, I missed you."

"A, get this recorded, because Ivy Blackthorn *actually* missed somebody," Nate cried, and we all burst out laughing.

"Jeez, you make me out to be a heartless bitch," Ivy retorted before shrugging the thought off.

Deep down, she probably knew that she was.

"And I hope you missed *me*," I yelled at her, trying to remind them that I was there too.

"Oh, yeah. That's right," Nate remarked, turning his head toward Ivy. "I heard that you left town for a year. How come? Had you left to come up with some master plan of yours?" Nate snickered, though Ivy was silent and sending him a death glare.

"*No*, I had decided to visit family back in Paris. I needed a break from this boring town."

"Since when do you have family in *Paris*? You can't

even speak French–"

"Why am *I* the only one who has to stay stuck in this miserable town? Everyone else gets to escape and visit places that I've always wanted to go to!" I cried, cutting Nate off before he could start an argument with Ivy.

"Hey, maybe when we graduate, we can take a road trip and visit a bunch of places around the world together," Nate suggested, and I liked the idea a lot.

"Yeah," Ivy agreed. "But, for now, you know what we should do?" She paused dramatically, looking at us as if we should have known the answer. "We should *celebrate*!"

"Celebrate? What are we celebrating, exactly, on a Tuesday evening?" I questioned, leaning back against the steps.

Ivy always tried to find excuses for us to get together and drink, even if it wasn't because of something big – play rehearsals; test results above sixty percent; holidays; international STEM Day, which we still didn't quite get the meaning behind.

"The beginning of junior year? My and Ivy's arrival back in town? All of us together again?" Nate exclaimed, counting off on his fingers. "Come on, A! Catch up!"

I sighed, deciding to give in. "All right, then. I'm down. The graveyard at seven o'clock it is."

It was an extraordinarily bizarre place to meet and drink. But somehow, we had always found it more relaxing than creepy in the town's graveyard. Maybe it had to do with the fact that a lot of people that we had loved were buried there – Ivy had lost her father at a young age; I had lost both

Annabeth and my father; Nate had lost a cousin a while back that had committed suicide.

The black metal gate squeaked loudly as we pushed by to enter after Ivy had picked the lock with a hairpin. Then, since I hadn't done so in a while, I asked for a few minutes alone and wandered down the rows of gravestones.

After coming upon the M Section, I kneeled in front of the tombstone reading, *"Jack Morgenstern: Loving Father and Husband."*

My father passed away at the end of eighth grade. He had been a healthy, kind, warm-hearted man who had done *nothing* wrong. After I had come back from the middle school dance, though, I found my mother shaking and in tears on the phone. She then told me that my father had mysteriously vanished from work. His olive-green Jeep had disappeared from the parking lot, and no matter who contacted him – the office, his friends, my mom – there had been no reply.

After evenings booked with countless search parties, we hadn't been able to find anything. That was until his car had shown up, about a week later, crushed by a lamppost and engulfed in flames.

It was then stated to have been a car crash.

An accident.

But I had never believed the statement for a minute. My father had to have been in *much* more trouble to have disappeared like that. They never even found the body.

Just reliving the painful memories gave me goosebumps. I tried to remember why I had been at my dad's tombstone until it clicked, and I began digging through my messy school bag to find the bouquet that I had brought for him. It was made up of daisies that were dyed blue and green.

"I love you," I whispered as I placed down the bouquet before walking away.

I didn't know what else to say.

I found my way back to my friends, who were sitting on a bench with open beer cans already in their hands. I sat down in between them and took a sip from the cold can that Nate handed me. We then sat in silence, staring up at the starry, clear sky.

"*This* is boring," Ivy cried not even a minute after, huffing before she took a huge gulp of beer. "Oh, I know. How about we play the classic game of one-on-one Truth?"

The Truth Game had been a favorite of ours back in ninth grade. Over the years, we had gotten so good that we would tell each other *everything*.

The goal was simple: The first person to get caught lying within a round of two minutes would lose.

It was an effortless way of spilling all your secrets.

"Sure," Nate and I agreed, and a mischievous smile crept up my face.

"Ready?" Ivy asked me after she finished playing The Truth Game against Nate – and winning.

I nodded before playing a round of Rock, Paper, Scissors against her to see who would go first. Ivy lost with rock since I chose paper, so I began to think of a plan.

Of course, with Ivy, there were many questions that I could ask her that she wouldn't want to answer truthfully. The ones that suddenly came to mind, though, were *perfect.*

I started easy as Nate began the timer on his phone. "Have you ever been arrested?"

"Sweetie, it's *me* that you're asking. Get a little more creative – ask me something *deeper.*" She had this sly grin on her face that drove me crazy as she talked. "But, *fine.* No, I have never been arrested, and you should know that. After all, you would have been the first person that I would have asked to bail me out." I rolled my eyes as she laughed. "*Now*, have you ever slept with someone?"

"*No*, you haven't been gone for *that* long," I grumbled, feeling my face burn.

It wasn't like I had dated anyone since Nate. I hadn't been able to bring myself to do it.

"I saw that answer coming," Ivy remarked after glancing at Nate with a smirk.

Had they really placed a *bet* on that question?

Anger bubbling inside of me at the thought, I decided that it was time to ask what I had been really curious to know. "Where were you the night of Annabeth Landers' murder?"

"What kind of question is that?" Ivy hissed, narrowing her eyes at me. "I don't know. I had just gotten back from Paris and was probably out drinking with some friends."

"Since when do *you* have other friends?" I asked her bitterly, confused by her alibi.

"And since when do *you* have permission to ask another question?" she bit back, shutting me up. "*My* turn. Why did you *really* like Annabeth Landers? Was it only because of the social hierarchy standards that she helped you reach–?"

"I liked Anna because she was a nice person who always stuck by my side and didn't *move away*," I responded as calmly as I could, though Ivy was getting on my nerves.

"I wouldn't call her *nice*..." Ivy began but trailed off.

"Then what *would* you call her? I mean, you were *apparently* friends."

"I would call her a selfish *bitch* who always wanted her way. She always wore that perfect persona and had *everyone* fooled. Even *you*, for that matter." Ivy took another sip from the can in her hand. "And we *weren't* ever friends – I have no clue who you heard that bullshit from."

"Ethan," I mumbled, hoping that Ivy hadn't heard. By the smirk on her face, though, I noticed that she had.

"Well, he doesn't know shit, does he?" Ivy played with a lock of her dark hair. "Now, if you *couldn't* have Nate, who would you date? Let's be real – nobody could go two years without wondering that."

The question took me aback, and I went silent. I had to think of something, *anything*, besides the honest answer – *Ethan.*

"Time," Nate stated, saving my ass and ending the round. "Wow, *that* was a crazy game," he added, completely unaware of how tense Ivy and I now were.

"Yeah," I sighed, taking in a gulp of frigid air. "I'm gonna go take a walk, actually – get ready for the next round." Without looking to see if they were okay with it, I walked away from our bench.

I wandered down the rows, this time looking for

Annabeth's tombstone. It had only been a week since the funeral, yet it had felt like an eternity since I'd visited. The tombstone still looked the same – not that it *could* change – throwing off a damp smell like sadness and broken dreams.

I didn't know what to do. I felt as if I should apologize for everything, even when I knew that she probably couldn't hear. Before I could, though, fog began crawling on the ground, clouding my sight. A flash of red – *blood* – blinded my vision. My head began to burn as if something was straining my thoughts. I fell to the floor, holding my head in pain until my vision became clear again.

However, the tombstone in front of me wasn't Anna's anymore. At least, it didn't seem to be since all her information had been erased, only leaving an engraved message behind.

Don't trust anyone, or you will pay the cost.
And your life may be the lowest price.

I was frozen in place, terrified as I stared down at the message. I reread it in my head.

Who would say such things? Is Anna's ghost out to get me for what I've done, or is she warning *me about what I don't know–?*

A shriek sounded from beneath me as a pale, cold hand with ruby-painted nails sprung from the ground in front of the grave. It grabbed my ankle tightly, and a burning pain coursed through my leg until I was able to shake the hand loose.

I stumbled back onto Nate. "What is it? Are you

okay?" Nate questioned as Ivy came to join him. "We heard you scream."

I was panting, and my heart was racing so fast that I thought that I was having a heart attack. "There was-was a message and a-a hand trying to-to pull me underground, and–"

"What are you *talking* about, A? There's nothing here," Ivy stated, staring at me as if I was a psychopath. "I think you just drank too much. Come on, let's get you home."

They tried to pull me away from the tombstone, and reluctantly, I obeyed but managed to look back. And as I did, I noticed that Anna's tombstone was back to normal. The exaggerated amount of fog had disappeared, and so had the message and the hand.

It was as if nothing had ever happened.

Chapter 12
Jessi
A Cut Too Deep to Heal

W hat the hell am I doing here?

I stared up at the gym doors in all their dented, dull blue glory as my legs started to shake.

"Jess!" Only one voice I knew had that sweet, slightly sharp tone like rock candy – Annabeth.

I whirled around, my teal duffel bag slamming against my hip. There was Anna, wearing her orange, phoenix-emblazoned school jersey. It had a small number twenty-two stitched on the front and a larger copy of the number printed on the back in gold.

"Why are you just standing out here?" Anna asked, sounding bewildered. "Tryouts are going to start soon."

I shrugged, trying to seem nonchalant but failing. I started to chew anxiously at my nails.

"Why are you nervous?" Anna questioned, crossing her arms over her chest.

"I'm not nervous," I lied, not making eye contact with her.

Anna rolled her eyes. "You're chewing your nails like a rodent." She tossed her long, curly ponytail over her shoulder. "But really, you don't have to worry. You'll do great."

My cheeks turned hot at the comment, and slowly I began to feel better about myself – if Anna thought I was good, then I had to be.

Before I could tell her how amazing she was, though, Anna's expression shifted. She looked me up and down, shaking her head like a disappointed teacher. "However, you're not leaving your hair like that."

"Wh-Why not?" I sputtered, tugging on the section of my hair that I had draped over my right eye to conceal my birthmark. "It's better off this way."

"You'll trip with all that hair blocking your view," Anna pointed out, then sighed. "Now, come on. I'll braid your hair before warm-ups."

I started to protest, but Anna was already heading into the gymnasium, dragging me along. Once we entered, she set down her pearly-pink Lululemon duffel bag, then motioned for me to turn around. Reluctantly, I obeyed.

Annabeth's fingers started sifting through my thick hair, sectioning it, and my face went hot again. Once Anna twisted my short, messy hair into a surprisingly neat plait, she pulled a black elastic from her wrist and tied off the braid. "There," she remarked, turning me back around. "Isn't that better?" She then caught a glimpse of my flushed face and frowned. "Stop being so embarrassed. You look good."

"Um, sure," I responded, willing my face to go back to its normal shade.

Both Anna and I stared at each other for a few awkward seconds. Then, Anna cleared her throat and looked at the line of girls slowly heading outside. "Well, come on, Little J! We're running the track," she stated. She pointed toward the back doors of the gymnasium, which opened to the side of the school where there were a soccer field and a gravel track.

"Right," I replied, following Anna to the doors and feeling a little dazed.

Why did she just stare at me back there? Did I say something wrong? Or could she have been nervous?

I looked at Anna, who was back to her normal, confident self. The afternoon sunlight made her blonde curls shine, and I wondered if her face looked a little bit flushed—

I crashed into the door, then blinked.

The door wasn't open, it wasn't sunny, and I was alone.

I shook my head, then backed away from the door. A few girls were looking at me and snickering.

Anna's not here.

I stared at the gym floor, cursing myself for getting caught up in the past. It was hard when I was attempting to make the school's volleyball team *just* for her, and now was the first round of tryouts.

I have to keep it together, I told myself. *For Anna.*

After a few quick stretches and the roll call, our coach, Ms. Brynn, told us to start a game. We got into formation, splitting into two groups. I suddenly realized that I had forgotten to put on my knee pads but decided that it didn't matter – I didn't feel like I had enough energy to participate like I usually did.

This was going to be my first game without Anna. I *knew* that. Yet it felt like she was still there, standing beside me as she tightened her ponytail with that determined look of hers on her face.

"Don't look so nervous, Little J!" Anna would have scolded as she got into her ready position. "You want to *scare* the opponents, not make them feel more confident about themselves." I tried to tear my gaze away from the image of Anna across from me, focusing on the other team, who was preparing to serve. "Come on, Little J! This serve is all yours."

Stop it, Anna! I mentally screamed. *Stop it!*

"Pay attention! You've got this!"

Shut up! You're not real!

"Hey! Watch out!"

I blinked.

I was now on the floor, and my left cheek was stinging.

I had missed the serve.

I looked up, expecting the disappointed faces of my teammates–

There stood half a dozen Annabeths, who were looking down at me and wearing expressions ranging from concern to mockery.

"Miss Alvarez?" one of them said in my coach's voice. "Are you all right?"

"Yeah, you good?" another one asked with her

hands on her hips. She sounded a lot like Marrisa Langford –
the volleyball team captain.

"Stay *away* from me!" I screamed, stumbling up from
my place on the floor. "You're not real – you're *dead*!"

All the Annabeths looked at each other, confused.

"Jessi, what the hell–"

"No!" I cried, cutting off an Annabeth who sounded
like Kristen Decker. I then walked to the door with my head
down, though I could hardly focus on what I was looking at.

Not wanting to stay around any longer, I grabbed my
duffel bag from off the bench that was closest to me. I darted
out of the gymnasium and down the twisty hallways, feeling
as if I was trying to escape a never-ending maze.

I can't do this. I have to get out of here.

Finally, the front doors came into view. I picked up
my pace, eager to escape–

I caught the toe of my shoe on a pointy edge of the
patch of broken tiles near the front entrance of the school,
sending myself sprawling. I landed hard on a particularly
sharp piece of tile, scraping my left knee and palm.

"Crap," I mumbled, staring at the blood. I then wiped
it away on my black gym shorts before standing back up. I
fixed the strap of my duffel bag over my shoulder and
carefully walked out the door of the school. As I managed to
catch my breath, though, I suddenly felt as if all the air had
been knocked out of my lungs.

A few feet away, I spotted Adley sitting next to Nate
at one of the picnic tables. Nate was holding her hand – and
Ivy was sitting across from them with a wide smirk.

I dashed into the parking lot and ducked behind a

nearby car, trying to quiet my breathing so that I wouldn't grab anyone's attention. I blinked hard, hoping that what I was seeing was all in my head.

But it wasn't.

What the hell? Why is Adley hanging out with Nate and Ivy again? Did she really choose the asshole who broke her heart and Anna's possible killer?

Peeking around the car that I was hiding behind, I watched Ivy, Nate, and Adley, who were laughing and bantering like old friends. I sank to the hot pavement, trembling.

Everything was so screwed up.

I was so screwed up.

Adley's hanging out with Ivy again.

I'm seeing things.

Annabeth is gone, and she isn't coming back.

"Shut up," I whispered to myself, trying to quiet the thoughts that were buzzing around like hornets in my head.

I slowly stood up, wincing as my cut knee burned. I walked through the parking lot in a daze, then sat down on the curb that was out of the Terrible Trio's sight. After stretching out my injured leg, I noticed that the cut wasn't super deep. But with all the running that I had done, twin trickles of blood dripped down my leg, staining the top of my white sock. I knew that I wouldn't be able to walk all the way home, even if I took a shortcut through the town square. Plus, all the school buses had left already, the nearest bus stop was still quite a while away, and my dad was at work.

I could only think of one more option.

I pulled my phone out of my duffel bag and slowly started to dial. "Ethan?"

I had never been so happy to see a car in my entire life.

As soon as the silver GMC came to a halt, Ethan leaped out of the passenger side. He came running over to me, his face twisted in concern. While I had been sitting on the curb, it started to rain lightly. So, in only my Ember Falls Phoenixes jersey and black shorts, I was shaking like a leaf. The rain had also smeared the blood from my scrape, so my leg looked like I had painted it with red watercolor paint.

Ethan sat beside me on the curb, the tiny raindrops darkening his light gray hoodie. "Jessi, what *happened* to you?"

I met his concerned-looking brown eyes, feeling mine fill with tears. "I tried, Ethan," I rasped, pulling my knees to my chest. "I tried to make the team for Anna. But I couldn't."

Ethan's face crumpled. "Oh, Jessi."

"I'm sorry," I whispered, feeling tears slip from my eyes.

Ethan didn't say anything back, his own eyes shiny as he helped me off the ground. His mom was standing by the car, and her eyes widened when she saw me leaning helplessly against Ethan, dragging my duffel bag on the wet pavement.

"I'm sorry," I apologized, this time to Mrs. Landers. I positioned myself in the backseat as she got into the driver's side. "This must be *super* inconvenient–"

"Please, don't worry about that," Mrs. Landers said

as Ethan walked around the car and came to sit on the other side of me. "I'd much rather come to pick you up than have you walk home like *that*."

"What *did* happen?" Ethan asked gently, fastening his seatbelt after slamming the car door shut next to him.

I laughed softly, but it didn't sound as light and happy as I had wanted it to. "Ember Falls High needs new tiles."

No one made any comments. I nervously twirled my charm bracelet around my wrist, fingering a small amethyst crystal that I had recently clipped on it. My eyes dropped to the floor then, and I noticed a piece of paper near my feet. I reached down to grab it and recognized it immediately. Written with green ink, in Ethan's less-than-neat handwriting, was Annabeth's poem.

"Oh, *that's* where that went," Ethan exclaimed, looking at the sheet as if he wanted to rip it from my hands.

"I didn't know that you made a copy," I said softly, reading over the familiar poem.

"Yeah, I gave the original to Adley." Ethan's face went red before his eyes widened with surprise. "Wait, you knew about the poem?"

"Um, yeah." It was my turn to blush. "I saw it when Adley was reading it one day." When Ethan didn't say anything, I added, "It's really good, isn't it?"

"It is." A sad smile spread across his face. "I think it's about Adley."

I felt my heart sink. Most of it *had* seemed to be about Adley, but a tiny part of me had wondered if, *maybe*, some of it had been about *me*.

If Anna's brother thought it was about Adley, though, it probably was.

"Of course," I whispered, barely audible.

Ethan shrugged as he gazed out the window. "There is one part that doesn't really make sense – the part about singing in the rain. But I think that's just, you know, poetry. I mean, Adley doesn't sing, nor does she like rain, but it's the thought that counts, I guess."

In the window's reflection, I could see that Ethan was getting that silly look on his face – the same look that he always got when he talked about Adley. It made me smile a little.

Suddenly, the look faded from his face, getting replaced with something that looked like heartbreak. I leaned forward to look out the window, trying to get a glimpse of what had made him react the way that he had–

Slowly disappearing behind us was the Toxic Three. And even though they were blurry through the rain-splattered window, I could tell that Adley and Nate were in an intense lip-lock.

"Ethan, I...." I started, biting my bottom lip as I tried to find something to say. "They...."

Ethan tore his gaze away from the window, heartbreak slowly shifting into something that looked like anger. His hands balled into loose fists. "It's fine," he mumbled, glancing down at his black Converse.

That was everyone's favorite catchphrase nowadays.

Chapter 13
Adley
The Downward Spiral

I can't *believe* you!"

"Well, what else am I supposed to say?"

"I don't know. I'm not the *parent*!" I screamed. I marched into the kitchen and threw my school bag onto a high stool at the kitchen island.

My mom stood across from me, her eyes wide in astonishment at the words that had flown out of my mouth. "Of course, you aren't. That's *my* job."

"Wow, it *is*?" I laughed bitterly, not caring how pissed my mom would be afterward – if she'd even care, that was. "You know, sometimes, I can never tell. You're not here three-quarters of the time; my friend died, and you didn't care to ask me how I felt; when I broke up with Nate, instead of talking to me, you left for a week on a business trip and didn't call–" I was running out of breath just listing the disappointments. "Now, I committed an act of felony, and all you say is, 'okay'?"

"Your teacher had only called this morning to advise me of what happened yesterday. She said that she would cover it up if you and that trouble-making friend of yours don't try this stunt again," my mom explained as she sat down at the dining room table. She opened a *Vogue* magazine and began reading one of the articles as she sipped from her "Best Mom Ever" coffee mug.

Yesterday, on the school grounds, Ivy and I had been standing where the gravel track and soccer field had ended and a whole forest had begun. There had been no people in sight since it was a Thursday afternoon – an extracurricular-free day at our school – meaning that we were completely alone.

School had ended, and Ivy and I had snuck into the art room to steal a few cans of spray paint. We had never been artistic people, but I had so much anger bubbling inside of me from *Jessi* that I was in major need of this.

So, we found a spot, laid out our assortment of colored cans, then began to draw on the trunk of a nearby tree. On one side, Ivy had been in the middle of a full-blown masterpiece with her name written in huge, green bubble letters. I, on the other hand, had been staring intensely at my side of the tree, not knowing what to do.

"What did I ever do to Jessi Alvarez?" I had thought aloud as Ivy stopped drawing and laughed before I could continue ranting.

"You didn't do *anything*. She's just a child who can't move on without causing a little drama. Come on, you were only friends because of Annabeth. And now that she's gone, Jessi doesn't know what to do." Ivy had looked away from me and gone back to spray painting the tree. "Look, forget about her, and remember the people who are *much* better."

I had known that Ivy was referring to herself and Nate. But somehow, I had only found myself thinking about Ethan.

But what had been the point? If Jessi had decided to move on, then I had a strong feeling that Ethan wouldn't stay around for much longer either.

Not that I would have blamed him.

A rush of anger had then consumed me. I had begun to rage-paint, spraying line after line all over the innocent tree trunk until it was covered in a design resembling a childish drawing of a spiderweb. I then dropped the cans onto the floor afterward, staring at my masterpiece.

All until I had heard footsteps coming from behind and was spooked, alongside Ivy. It had turned out to be the art teacher, Mrs. Marin – and she looked *mad*.

"What on Earth are you girls *doing*?" she had cried, ruffling the maroon curls that were draped over her shoulders. Her eyes had then fallen upon the spray cans, and I knew that we were dead.

Mrs. Marin had ended up sparing us, knowing that we were going through rough times ever since Annabeth's death. If we were to have done it again, though, she'd get the police involved. We *had* gotten stuck with a week of detention after school, however, starting the following Monday.

"Had *only called*?" I repeated loudly, resuming the fight. "Mom, I could have gotten *arrested*. Where's your head?" I then found it lost in an article reading, "Fall Fashion: The Dos and Don'ts," which I pulled out from under my mother's hands.

"Then, what should I do?"

"*Punish* me? *Talk* to me?" I stated as I paced back and forth in front of the table. "I can tell that it was always *Dad* who took care of this stuff—"

"*Fine*, if raising yourself sounds so easy, why don't you try it? I won't make your meals, I won't do your laundry, and you can forget about getting an allowance for the chores you do," my mother declared, glaring at the magazine tucked under my arm.

"It's not like you've been doing any of *that* for the past three years." I sighed, combing a hand through my curls. "Admit that ever since Dad died, you haven't been able to be there for anybody else *but* yourself. The last time that you were present in our lives was for Caleb's high school graduation." A tear slipped from my eye, and I quickly wiped it away. "I'd be surprised if you even show up at *mine*." Without giving my mother time to comment, I picked up my school bag from its spot on the chair and stormed off toward the front door.

"Adley," my mom began as I threw on my coat.

"Save it! I have to get to school," I exclaimed before walking out the door and slamming it shut behind me.

My tears finally dried by the time I crossed paths with Ethan on the way to school. Oddly, this time, Ethan didn't even try to join me. He just walked unhurriedly on the opposite side of the vacant street.

I decided to jog over, needing someone to distract me. "Hey," I called as I joined him and slowed my pace.

"Oh, hi," he replied, though he didn't meet my eyes. "So, I heard that Nate and Ivy are back in town."

"Yeah, it's weird having them back, honestly. Jessi has been acting weird about it, and... so are *you.*"

Ethan's face reddened, and his gaze fell to the floor. "Me? I'm not at all. You can hang out with whomever you want. I can't speak for Jessi, though. She hates your friends and doesn't try to hide it."

I laughed. "Oh, I know. And whatever happens between me and Jessi, is between me and her. I don't want it to ruin our friendship."

"Yeah, *friendship,*" Ethan mumbled under his breath. He then looked back up and stopped walking, so I came to a halt.

There, in front of us, was the graveyard. We passed it every morning, so it wasn't like I was petrified of its sight. It was just eerier than usual and oddly had smoke spewing out of its opened gate – exactly like the last time I had visited.

Intrigued and curious to know where the smoke was coming from, I left Ethan's side. I then crossed the street quickly and took off into the fog.

"Adley?" I could hear Ethan call from behind. "Adley, we need to get to school. Get out of there or–" His voice then stopped, either because he had cut himself off, or because I couldn't hear him any longer.

I treaded through the yard, looking around curiously as I tried to see where the smoke started. Was it some kind of machine? Minutes later, though, I realized that the smoke had created some kind of *trail* – and it had led me to Anna's grave.

This time, however, the gravestone had dramatically *changed*. Pieces of the tombstone had crumbled and broken off, there was red spray paint all over the grave, and there were fresh, muddy footprints that were bigger than my own.

"Adley?" I heard Ethan's voice call again, this time getting louder with every syllable until I stubbled into him. "Adley, what are you doing…?" He trailed off as he fell upon the sight of his sister's tombstone. His eyes widened in shock, and he took a step back, shaking his head in disbelief. "What the *hell*?"

"I saw this huge cloud of fog, so I decided to follow it, and–"

"*What* cloud of fog?" Ethan questioned, sounding concerned as he turned in a circle to look around. "I don't see anything."

I was puzzled.

Doesn't Ethan see the gloomy gray sky, the muddy grass, and the never-ending cloud of thick fog?

I shrugged the thought off, trying to convince myself that I wasn't hallucinating again. "My point is, after walking around, I came upon *this*."

Ethan kneeled in front of the grave and began to pick up the crumbled pieces of stone, which he threw into a pile on his left.

I dropped to his side, carefully trying not to get my ripped jeans covered in mud. I then glanced at my phone to check the time. "Well, it's only eight o'clock. I suppose we've got some time to pick this up," I stated as I started to help Ethan with his stone collecting.

When I came upon a piece of stone that had rolled behind the tombstone, though, I walked over to get it—

I spotted another creepy warning on the back of Anna's tombstone, and a chill rolled down my back. It was written in red paint, which matched what the stone had been sprayed with.

Watch out, bitch! You may be next.

When I blinked, though, the sky was blue, the birds were chirping, the muddy ground was dry, and the message was gone.

Along with my sanity.

Chapter 14
Jessi
We All Knew This Day was Coming

I *had to run.*

I wasn't sure where to, but I knew that I needed to get there. It was like something was pulling me, leading me through the smoky darkness that obscured my vision. I kept running blindly, trusting whatever was guiding me.

Eventually, my pace began to slow. My eyes seemed to adjust to the darkness, giving me the ability to make out where I was.

The Ember Falls graveyard.

Part of me screamed to turn around and run far away. But I was frozen in place, staring at Annabeth's headstone – and at Annabeth herself.

She was standing beside her grave, dressed in her torn lilac nightgown, hands clasped in front of her. Her eyes had a strange glow to them like a cat's eyes under a light, and her face was expressionless.

But she was there, whole and alive.

I tried to run to her – to call her name – but it was like I was a statue. I was stiff and rooted to my spot in the grass.

Anna, I'm right here, I tried to scream, but nothing came out of my mouth. It was as if I was muted.

Suddenly, a hand that seemed to be made of darkness crept up Anna's shoulder. A tall shadow loomed over her, its eyes glowing red. "What a shame," it drawled in the same voice that had been haunting my dreams for weeks. "You're too late to save your precious little angel."

Then, as I watched helplessly, the shadow grabbed Annabeth and shoved her into the headstone, which cracked and shattered into a thousand pieces. Blood from the deep gash on her forehead dripped down onto the headstone, coating it in shiny red.

The shadow disappeared, fading into the distance, and I felt myself unfreeze. I sprinted toward Anna, desperately hoping that I could save her this time–

I slammed face-first into an invisible wall and stumbled backward. No matter how hard I pounded at it, it wouldn't break. I then watched from afar as life slowly bled out of Annabeth.

I couldn't help *her.*

I couldn't save *her.*

I will never be able to do anything but watch.

My nightmares eventually convinced me that I needed to visit Anna.

After school, I stood outside of the Ember Falls graveyard. My backpack's strap was slung across one shoulder, and I held a small bouquet against my chest. I had chosen two types of wildflowers – chicory for their bluish-lilac tone, and wild daisies for their delicate beauty.

I stared at the black metal fence that encased the graveyard, watching as a flake of paint peeled off and blew away in the wind. The area was deserted, and along with the cover of gray clouds, the graveyard looked doubly depressing. I leaned against a nearby tree, trying to keep my weight off my healing knee. I sighed tiredly, barely suppressing a yawn.

Every night, I hadn't been sleeping properly. In fact, I had been so sleep-deprived that I had fallen asleep in English class one morning, only to be jolted awake a few minutes later by an unhappy teacher. The dreams were the same every time, but they still terrified me. They were so *real,* and I would wake up feeling an indescribable terror – both for myself and Annabeth.

Then, there was that voice, always lingering in my thoughts like a song that was on a constant loop. Even during my waking hours, I would sometimes hear it, repeating the same line – I couldn't help but wonder if I could have saved Anna.

If I could've stopped all of this from happening…

Shoving the thoughts of my nightmares away, I took a deep breath and headed into the graveyard. I tried not to shiver as I walked down the alphabetized rows of headstones. When I came upon the L Section, I slowed my pace, counting gravestones until I found the spot that I knew was dedicated to Annabeth–

I dropped my bouquet.

No.

I blinked hard as if that would erase what was in front of me.

Anna's gravestone – *vandalized.*

It was exactly like it had been in my dream. Except for the fact that the blood had been traded out for angry red slashes of spray paint.

I kneeled in front of Anna's grave, staring at her disheveled tombstone in shocked silence.

Who could have done this? Who would *have done this?*

I reached out and gently touched the crumbling headstone. Tears of anger burned in my eyes. "Anna. Oh, my God... Who *did* this?"

Part of me expected to see Anna there, telling me what had happened. But I was all alone in the graveyard, the flowers from my bouquet scattered amongst the shattered granite like they were trying to hide the damage.

However, I already had a strong feeling about who was behind this – and I wasn't going to let her get away with it.

Back at the entrance of the graveyard, I stared into the sunset, waiting to see the familiar blue and red lights of police cars.

You're going to pay for this, Ivy.

I may not have had *solid* evidence to support my claim of her vandalism, but she was *Ivy Blackthorn* – she probably already had a history with the police. Either way, Ivy was suspicious as hell.

Maybe the police officers would catch her for good.

Maybe they would find more evidence on her, and she would finally end up behind bars.

Exactly where Annabeth's killer belongs.

In the distance, I could hear the wail of sirens. Instead of being annoying, they sounded like music – the soundtrack to Ivy's capture.

I watched eagerly as two police cars turned around the corner, heading for the graveyard. I started to mentally recite the speech that I had rehearsed, making sure to remember all the tiny details. The two cars stopped in front of me, their lights casting the street in a strange, flickering glow. I watched as a tall, familiar police officer stepped out of one of the cars, her frizzy ponytail billowing in the cool evening breeze.

Officer Roden.

Whatever, I thought, shaking off my uneasiness. *It doesn't matter. I'm not the guilty one here.*

Officer Roden approached me, and her face was unreadable.

"I have reason to believe," I started, "that Ivy Blackthorn is–"

Officer Roden held her hand up, silencing me. "*Please*, spare me the next part of your tall tale, Miss Alvarez," she said, her voice harsh in annoyance.

"What...?"

Officer Roden gestured to her car, and I followed her hand. I looked into the back of the vehicle and spotted Adley and Ivy. They were sitting inside, looking somewhere between angry and afraid. I suddenly understood Officer Roden's words.

It looked as if *I* had been a part of this. As if *I* had framed Ivy to cover up the crime that I committed.

Chapter 15
Adley
You Can't Hide from Who You Are

The police officers had finally found us for the spray-painted tree.

At least, that had been the first thought that crossed my mind when a roaring police car pulled up next to me and Ivy.

After the fight that morning with my mom, I had to get away from my house – mainly to prove my valid point that I didn't need my mother. Of course, I had forgotten that I needed a new place to stay. So, I had been very thankful when Ivy gave me the okay to stay at her apartment for a while.

In honor of our first night together, after we had ordered a large, all-dressed pizza and watched our favorite slasher film, *Scream*, we decided to go into town. We had fallen upon Andrew's Arcade and were only there for a few minutes before hearing police cars passing on Main Street. Curious, we exited, and that was when one of the cars pulled up next to us. The young woman had then explained from the driver's side that they were searching for Ivy after receiving new evidence that made her look guilty of murdering Annabeth.

For a second, I had thought that they believed that we vandalized Anna's tombstone. Especially when the police car had then driven to the cemetery, where Jessi the Saint was waiting with a smirk on her face. They had only learned about the vandalism then, though, and another investigation scene began to unfold as we watched from the car's back seat.

Jessi had been shoved into the back too, while she was explaining that she finally found the perfect evidence to rest the case that Ivy was Anna's murderer. That included having me testify because *I* was an accomplice.

I now sat uncomfortably still, trying to look calm and composed as if it was no big deal that I was in an interrogation room on a Friday night. I'd had the choice of having a guardian sit next to me throughout the session, but knowing that my only option was the woman who I wasn't on good terms with, I passed.

The attractive, blond-haired police officer that sat across from me, hands clasped in front of him on the table, stared into my eyes. Not to my surprise, my blood hadn't changed from the new test that they had conducted. That was making the police officer irritated but intrigued.

"What do you know about the night of Annabeth Landers' murder?" he asked bluntly as he tugged at the nametag reading "Officer Porter" on his navy-blue uniform top.

"I know that it *happened*," I began smoothly. "I was her *best friend,* after all." I faked a tear of sadness, which slid down my cheek and landed on my gray hoodie, hoping for sympathy. "That evening, I was in the house with her, along with her twin brother, Ethan, and Jessi Alvarez. Jessi and I were sleeping over."

"Play innocent," I heard a whisper say. At those words, Damion appeared right behind the police officer. Damion's hands were clasped behind his back as he leaned over the police officer's shoulders to peer at the notes being jotted down. Damion then gave me a warning look.

I knew that I *had* to play along.

"All I remember is waking up to Anna's mother screaming in horror at the sight of the body. I don't know anything that you don't." My voice became panicked, aiding me in my attempt to make my pain seem believable.

Somehow, the police officer fell for the act. "I'm so sorry, Miss Morgenstern. My sympathies," the officer said in a calmer voice. I nodded before wiping my watery eyes with a shaking hand. "Changing the subject, what are your ties to Ivy Blackthorn?"

"She's a close friend of mine. We've known each other since ninth grade. She and I used to always hang out, along with my boyfriend – Nathaniel Tucker. That was until she left a year ago to visit family in Paris, only getting back at the start of August."

"Are you aware that your friend has plenty of evidence, proving that she may have committed Miss Landers' murder? One included the vandalized tombstone."

"You believe that Ivy committed *that*?" I asked in disbelief. "She likes to play with spray paint, but Ivy wouldn't do such a thing. She doesn't even have a tie with Annabeth besides that they weren't the friendliest." I paused, trying to find a way for that to have *not* sounded bad. "That was ages ago, though, you know?"

"Well, new evidence says otherwise."

"*New* evidence?" I questioned as I remembered that the only other documentation that had been claimed was the blog post on TheTea.com.

"Yes. Miss Blackthorn had *also* seen Miss Landers on the night of her death."

I was confused.

As far as I knew, I had been the last to see Anna before I murdered her.

The memory of that night was still blurry. But I was able to recall how Anna hadn't been able to sleep once the lights were turned off and Jessi was sound asleep. Anna kept tossing and turning in her pink sleeping bag, which prevented me from sleeping. So, I decided to stay up with her, and we whispered about boys and the hilarious moments of that sleepover.

The memory was then fuzzy between that moment and the murder, though I remembered Anna saying that she was going to get a glass of water in the kitchen. I had offered to go with her, but she said that she would be fine on her own. The rest of that night was blurry until I woke up the next morning in my sleeping bag, hearing the cry of Mrs. Landers. It was as if I had blacked out — I only knew that I killed Anna since the faint memories of her death kept appearing in my head.

But what had happened to lead up to that? Had anyone else seen her before I killed her? It all remained a mystery to me.

However, the police officer had explained to me that they had *evidence* – Ivy Blackthorn's grimy fingerprints marking a part of Anna's lilac nightgown.

It didn't make sense. Not one bit of it did. Ivy had just gotten back from Paris the night of the murder – how could she have been able to visit Anna?

It doesn't make sense, I kept thinking as I sat patiently in the police station's lobby. *It doesn't make sense.*

But then again, the entire situation didn't.

"Adley!" I heard a voice call from behind. To my surprise, it wasn't Damion, who had vanished into thin air after I did his bidding. It was Nate, his hazel eyes full of concern as he ran my way and pulled me into a hug. "Are you okay? Did they hurt you? I'll talk to them and make sure that they know you're innocent–"

"Nate, I'm perfectly okay. I was just in to clarify that I had nothing to do with the murder." I then took a deep breath and sighed. "It's *Ivy* who isn't safe."

Nate and I then looked over at Ms. Blackthorn in her beige trench coat, who was yelling through the narrow hallway that Ivy was being pulled down. "You'll be hearing from my lawyer. I know she didn't do it!" she declared loudly.

At the words, which made my body tremble, Nate held me tighter. "Don't worry. This isn't your fault."

But it is, I wanted to scream. I *killed Annabeth Landers.*

But I couldn't say that.

Not *then.* Not *there.* Not *ever.*

"Once they find proof that Ivy wasn't involved, she'll be fine," Nate reassured me.

But with a blog report, a vandalized tombstone, *and* fingerprints? That was enough to keep her locked up for good. After all, with that amount of evidence, she *had* to have been involved somehow – there were no other explanations.

Jessi barged out of room eighteen, her eyes red and her hands formed into fists.

Seeing her made my emotions boil to the surface, and I felt my fists tighten. She was the main reason that I was there in the first place, after all. "Did you *really* have to do this?" I yelled at her from across the lobby. Nate's mouth fell open at my sudden burst of anger. "Did you *really* have to call the police to declare that Ivy had vandalized Anna's tombstone? You don't even know if she did it or not."

"*Me?* Why do you automatically think that *I* had to have done it?" Jessi challenged after marching over to me with her hands on her hips. But even she probably knew the answer to that dumb question.

"Because you were there at the cemetery, idiot," I spat, rolling my eyes. "Besides, you have always *hated* Ivy's guts. You've always *hated* my friends. You probably just wanted Ivy stuck in jail so that I could come running back to you since you can't admit how much you *miss* me."

"Oh, it's *always* about *Adley Morgenstern.*"

"Shut up! You're jealous of Nate, Ivy, *and* Annabeth. Admit that all you've ever wanted since grade nine was the attention of the *popular* kids. Why else did you want to spend *so* much time with me and Anna?"

Jessi flinched. Then, her expression transformed into anger, her cheeks flushing as red as a tomato. "Don't bring up Anna like that."

"*Why?* She's *dead*, and she's *never* coming back! You just have to accept that."

"You wouldn't understand," Jessi whispered under her breath, and I caught her shivering.

"*I* wouldn't understand? She was *my* fucking best friend, Jessi!" I shouted, tired of her acting like she was the only one who cared.

Jessi's wide eyes burned with anger. She walked toward me, now standing so close that I could hear her heart racing. "So, what if I *did* call the police, huh?"

"Well, *did you*?" I asked furiously, my temper rising.

"Maybe I *did* and maybe I *didn't,*" she stated in a teasing voice, making me want to strangle the truth out of her. The smirk on her lips displayed how she knew that she was getting to me, and I hated it.

"That's *enough!*" Nate cried, startling me and Jessi since we had never seen him this angry before. "I'm bringing you home, Adley."

"I can get *myself* home, thank you very much," I told him bitterly as I shook his hands off my arm. I then picked up my duffel bag – which Ms. Blackthorn had given me after the interrogation – from off the seat next to mine, fixing its strap over my shoulder. "Remember, though: *you* started this,

Little J. And when I want something, I don't stop for anyone or anything until I get it." I paused as I walked toward the police station exit. Then, I added, not looking back, "That's what Annabeth taught me."

I didn't have many options for where to stay for the night after Ivy was arrested. Her being gone removed her from the list, and Jessi was obviously not even *considered* for a split second. If I asked Nate, I knew he'd make me explain the entire situation first. And *after* I would do so, I knew he'd march me over to my mother's house to apologize – and I didn't want to back down from that fight.

So, I found my way to the steps of the Landers' house and made myself comfortable on their porch swing. I took out a blanket, a black pen, and an old green notebook from my duffel bag. Then, I began to plan what I would do with my night. I wanted to knock on the door and ask to stay inside, but I didn't want to ask for any more favors.

I *couldn't.*

I decided to write a letter to Annabeth. It was mainly to help myself cope and move on but to also tell Anna my side of the story. Maybe it would be possible for her ghost to read it – *if* my seeing her during the Ouija board game hadn't all just been in my head.

Dear Anna,

~~*How are you? It's been a while.*~~
~~*I can't believe that this was how your extraordinary life story had to end.*~~
God, I miss you so much! From the way you did

everything with style and ease, to how you made the sun come out on the stormiest days because of your bright smile. When you would walk into a room, everything would change – you would change everything.

I can't believe that we won't be able to graduate together like we've been dreaming to do all our lives.

I can't believe you won't be able to live your life by my side anymore.

There is so much that I've been wanting to tell you. Like how Nate Tucker is back in town and is dating me again – I think. Or how Jessi Alvarez was finally so guilty of something that she was pulled in for questioning by the police after your murder – along with Ivy, who is now arrested *since there's a lot of evidence proving that she killed* you.

But she couldn't have done it, right? It was me, and we both know it.

Not that I remember why – I would never have wanted to hurt you.

Maybe things were supposed to turn out this way, though. Is that what the universe was trying to tell me – that you weren't supposed to be in my life? I have no clue how that could be. After all, ever since you've been gone, my life has been falling apart like that clay sculpture I had made during art class in first grade. Remember that? It was supposed to be Belle, my favorite Disney princess at the time, but her arms kept falling off and crumbling into a million pieces.

I hope you remember. You're the only one that knows these stories – the only one who knows the real me.

Or, at least, I think you do…

I wanted to stop writing for a second to take a break. But then, anger consumed me, and I began to scribble aggressively in the notebook.

Dammit, Anna! I need you. I need you on this complicated-as-hell planet where nobody loves me like you did. And screw writing letters to the dead! You're never going to read this. YOU ARE DEAD, AND YOU'RE NEVER COMING BACK!

I just have to accept that.

I dropped my pen, my hand trembling. I then ripped the page from the book, crumbled the paper into a tiny ball, and shoved it into the pocket of my gray hoodie. I was in so much pain that I couldn't stop thinking of the only thing that could cure the pounding in my head.

Hastily searching through my duffel bag, I tossed items around until I came across the small pill bottle. The plastic cooled my warm hands, and I sighed. As I was about to open its cap, though, my elbow smacked a potted aloe plant, sending it crashing to the floor. I was able to get the four last pills in my hand as the front door opened.

Ethan walked out, his eyes wide with alarm at the sight of the broken pot.

But then, he saw my petrified face – *and* the pills.

"What in the world are you *doing*?" Ethan cried after closing the front door behind himself. "You take *two* pills, Adley – not *four*."

"Two isn't giving me enough relief from the pain," I stuttered through tears as Ethan joined me on the swing.

"So, you jumped to *four*?" he asked, rocking the swing gently back and forth with his feet. I shrugged, not meeting his eyes. "And the pain from what – *headaches*?"

I shook my head. "Pain... from Anna's death. From the things I *see* – the things I *hear*." I began to cry harder, my breath hitching no matter how hard I tried to calm down. "I'm not going insane. But these pills, they just make it all *better*..."

"Oh, Adley..."

I suddenly knew the truth. "I-I have a problem, Ethan, an-and I don't know who to *talk* to or how to *feel* better–"

"Hey, it's okay." Ethan cupped my shaking hands in his as I stared at the floor. "You have me. I'm just relieved to know why you have been acting so different this past month."

"Different?" Feeling Ethan's eyes on me, I slowly put the pills back into the bottle. Then, I dropped the container into my bag.

"Yeah. For starters, you're camping out on my *porch*–"

"Which I will explain tomorrow. It's a *very* long story," I told him, a small laugh escaping my lips.

"Okay," he chuckled softly as he brushed a strand of my hair out of my face and tucked it behind my ear. I felt my face go hot, and my heart leaped in my chest. "Well, we've also barely talked, and you've been fighting with your friend–"

"*Jessi* is *not* my friend. She never was," I admitted to Ethan, wiping the tears off my face. "She was always Anna's friend. And now that Anna isn't here, you, Ivy, and Nate are my friends."

Ethan nodded, registering the facts before saying, "That was my last point. Your ex is back, and now, you're…?"

"*Dating.* We're together again." My response came out sounding as if I hated how true the fact was. I licked my bottom lip, looking down at my black boots. "Sorry that it's only coming out now. I didn't want to have to tell you."

"It's okay. I've already seen you two together a few times," Ethan stated quietly. I glanced up in shock, and it was his turn to look at the wooden planks of the porch. "But why didn't you want to tell me?"

"Well, you know, because…" I trailed off as my stomach turned in circles. I shifted uncomfortably, my palms sweating and my heart beating rapidly. I took a deep breath. "Because I *know* you like me, Ethan. As more than just a friend."

An awkward silence hung over us as we looked to the ground. I felt my face burn, while Ethan's turned pink. My heart started beating faster, and *faster,* and *faster* as I knew what I wanted to say, but I didn't think I should, but–

"And *I* like you too." It came out like a squeak from a mouse, but I knew that Ethan heard it. "I like you, Ethan Landers. That's why I didn't want you to know about me and Nate. I don't know if he's *the one* like he thinks he is."

I was then in tears again, crying into my hands. I wanted to tell him *everything.*

But I couldn't.

Not *then*. Not *there*. Not *ever*.

And it *killed* me.

I was sweating harder now. My body didn't know if it should be cold from the chilly, 1 AM breeze or hot from the discomfort of the situation. Ethan sat there, speechless, as well, and I was *scared*.

Did I get this all wrong? Does he not have the feelings that I always thought he had for me–?

Ethan's lips touched mine. I closed my eyes at his touch, his hand holding my cheek as our cold fingers intertwined. I kissed him back, forgetting all about Nate – just for one minute.

One minute only.

Our lips then parted seconds later, both of us out of breath. "You know me too well," Ethan laughed as he backed away from me and stood up. "But you're with Nate–"

"Forget about Nate *just* for tonight," I found myself saying, no matter how wrong I knew it was. "I want to know what it feels like to be with you for *one* night. Tomorrow, everything can go back to normal between us as if nothing had ever happened. It'll be our little secret."

Ethan seemed hesitant for a moment as if considering the outcome. But then, he nodded in agreement, a small smile on his lips. "Do you think Anna would approve of us?"

The question made my smile widen as I thought back to every time Ethan had tagged along with me and Anna. Every time she had teased him about his liking me. "As much as she had pushed you aside, I've always had this feeling that she was shipping us."

I then got up and kissed him again before he pulled me inside the house and shut the door.

Chapter 16
Jessi
You've Got Baggage

Once the police officers had questioned you *twice*, you were screwed.

That was what *I* had learned since – considering all the pestering and searching that I suffered through the night I attempted to report Ivy – I, at least, *felt* screwed.

I hadn't wanted to involve my dad again since I didn't him to think that I had some sort of involvement in any criminal activities. So, I endured the questioning *alone*. I had started to regret that decision, though, when Officer Roden blatantly accused me of formulating a plan to keep any evidence away from myself. I hadn't had anyone to back me up. That's why my attempts at protesting my innocence had been pathetic, and the article on TheTea.com had not helped my case.

In the end, I managed to convince Officer Roden that I was innocent, and she let me go. Besides, the police had more interesting things to investigate – they found fingerprints on Anna's nightgown that were in a pattern that looked like someone had *violently* grabbed her.

And those fingerprints had been a perfect match with *Ivy's.*

The things you hear when you eavesdrop, I thought, staring blankly at the history PowerPoint that was projected at the front of the class. I hated how my marks had been slipping this entire year. Though I did good on the PSATs the year before, I knew the SATs would only be harder when I took them in a few months. And I needed a good test score to get into Lawrence University, one of the high-ranking liberal art colleges nearby.

I forced my eyes to stay open, though I was still incredibly tired after the stress I'd gone through a few nights ago with the interrogation. Plus, no matter how hard I tried, I couldn't shake those nightmares.

I jolted awake when I heard a pencil roll off a nearby desk and tumble to the ground behind me. I looked up and ahead to realize that it was Adley's red mechanical pencil, which had rolled next to Ethan's desk – the one in front of mine. Adley was diagonal to me and next to Ethan. So, I had a clear view of her blushing and leaning forward to pick it up. But since it was in the middle of the row, Ethan also attempted to pick it up. It was when they both leaned down to pick up the pencil that they bumped heads, then both laughed, blushing.

I wanted to throw up at the sight.

I attempted not to display my disgust, looking down at my notebook. After her whole getting-back-together with Nate, I couldn't *believe* that she was attempting to play

Ethan. At least, that was what she seemed to be doing since all the blushing was out of the ordinary for her.

Is she trying *to make him even more miserable?*

I remembered the heartbroken look on Ethan's face when he had seen Adley and Nate kissing outside his car's window. I knew that Ethan would *always* give Adley another chance, no matter how many times she crushed him. But I was worried that he would just end up devastated.

I couldn't judge Ethan's decisions, though. Especially since I would probably have done the same thing, had Anna been asking me for a chance...

Not that I would have ever *gotten* that chance, even if she was alive.

I didn't deserve it.

I ducked through the crowded hallway after third period, keeping my head down. I stared down at my untied, white Converse, debating whether I had the energy or the willpower to tie them—

I crashed into someone, then stumbled backward, disoriented. I looked up at the person, planning to apologize, until I saw *who* it was.

I didn't know what to say.

Drake made me feel a mix of anger and shame, which boiled up inside me.

I shoved past him without so much as an "excuse me." I knew that I shouldn't have been so rude to him. But without Anna as a reason, I couldn't bear talking to him – not after what I had done.

It had been a stupid decision – a spontaneous thing

that I had done in a moment of anger and hotheadedness.

That doesn't change how badly it hurt Anna, though...

I had been sixteen and just about to go into eleventh grade – and probably at the peak of my stupidity. The gang had met up for Ethan's soccer game that August. But for me, that night had been more than just a standard summer's evening.

I had planned on *finally* telling Anna how I felt about her *that night.*

It had taken a while for me to build up the courage to decide to do it, but Anna didn't have a boyfriend at that time. I had told myself that I *needed* to say something then, or I would lose my chance.

So, when Annabeth had said that she needed to go to the washroom during the game's intermission, I took that as an opportunity to catch her alone. I followed her as she headed toward the small brick building in the park where the washrooms were, trying to stay out of site.

Something had been strange, though – Anna didn't even go into the washroom. She had just snuck past the building before looking over her shoulder as if she was afraid of being followed. Then, she pulled out her iPhone and typed a frantic message.

I had been about to reveal myself and ask if she was okay – start up a conversation before I dropped the I-Like-You-as-More-Than-Just-a-Friend bombshell. But then, a tall figure stepped out from the shadows, illuminated by the dim park lights.

I had only been able to make out the back of the

person, and I had never hated the back of someone's head so much. The person had short, messy dark hair and was wearing an Ember Falls High football jersey.

Anna's face lit up. She had thrown herself into the person's arms, saying their name with so much bliss that it hurt to listen to. *"Drake."*

I had stayed hidden behind a nearby tree, watching with teary eyes as Anna kissed the stranger, again, and *again, and again–*

Something inside me had suddenly snapped. At that moment, I decided that I couldn't bear to lose Annabeth to a boy.

Not again.

So, in a haze of rage and sadness, I had done something of which I *really* wasn't proud. Over the next month and a half, I had done everything that I could to break them up. I wished that I could say that I had just complained to Anna about her taste in partners, but I did so much worse.

It had been too easy. Drake was one of the popular kids – someone who always had more than one person fawning over him. Creating false evidence of him cheating on Annabeth hadn't been extremely hard – a note here, a whisper there.

I had felt *awful* about going through with it. Anna loved people's attention, and people loved her. So, having someone cheat on her had been the worst thing that a person could do to her – and I knew that.

That hadn't stopped selfish, sixteen-year-old me, however.

The worst thing was that even though my plan had

succeeded, I was never able to bring myself to say anything to her. I hadn't felt like I had a right to love her anymore.

Eventually, after enough of Drake's begging, Anna had taken him back. Then, I had been back to watching from afar and repeating the same thing to myself.

You don't deserve her.

After what felt like the longest trek from school in history, I dragged myself up the porch stairs and fished for my house key in my chaotic school bag. In my search, I pulled out a pair of busted earbuds, my battered copy of *The Hunger Games* – that I had read about a thousand times – an empty lip balm container, then – *finally* – my key.

Stepping into the house, I noticed that it smelled like coffee and cinnamon, which was odd. Dropping my bag by the entrance table, I headed into the kitchen. To my surprise, I found my dad sitting at the table with a beige mug of his usual coffee – the same overly-sweet cinnamon-and-cream concoction that I loved. He had his paperwork spread out in front of him, and his phone was pressed to his ear. I waved at him, and he waved back, smiling before turning back to his papers.

I wandered over to the kitchen cabinet and pulled out a tall glass. I set it on the counter, then rummaged through the fridge for something to drink. I pulled out a glass pitcher of iced tea and started pouring some into my glass, focusing hard so that I wouldn't spill it–

I heard my dad sigh and looked up, watching as he scribbled something onto a form. "Of course, I understand. I can guarantee you that I will do all that I can for you and your daughter, Ms. Blackthorn."

I stopped breathing.

Blackthorn? As in Ivy *Blackthorn?*

My father *could not* be Ivy's lawyer. I *refused* to believe it.

I felt something wet soak my white socks. I realized that I had never stopped pouring my iced tea and had overflowed my glass onto the floor. "Crap," I mumbled under my breath.

My dad looked up at me and made a face, halfway between concerned and annoyed. I mouthed "sorry" and bent down to the floor to clean up my mess.

My father is Ivy's lawyer.

I had heard Ivy's mother shouting at the police station that the police officers would be hearing from her lawyer. But I had never put two and two together.

I had never even *considered* the possibility.

My father is Ivy's lawyer.

Once I finished mopping up the spill with a few pieces of paper towel, I stood up, trembling.

What should I do now?

I suddenly felt dizzy, and the walls of my house seemed like they were caving in on me.

I have to get out of here.

Quickly, I scribbled a note on a scrap piece of paper that I had found discarded on the counter, making up some lame excuse about going to meet up with Adley. Then, nearly tripping over my feet in my haste, I headed out the door. Once I was far enough from my house, though, I started to run, letting the cool air nip at my cheeks as I tried to forget.

Maybe, if I tried hard enough, this whole thing would be a nightmare – a figment of my imagination.

Maybe, if I tried hard enough, I could wake up or snap out of it.

And *maybe*, when I did, Annabeth would be there, Nate would be long gone in New York City, everyone would be friends again, and I would never have to see Ivy ever again.

Maybe, just *maybe*.

Yet again, I found myself in a tree. Not that it was the worst way to cope with things, but I knew that there wouldn't always be a tree to climb when things went wrong.

I rolled an acorn between my palms, leaning back against a branch and staring at the pinkening sky.

My father is Ivy's lawyer.

I didn't know what I was supposed to do. I couldn't tell my dad *not* to take the case. That would never fly, especially if it was coming out of the mouth of a seventeen-year-old. However, I knew that I would go insane, watching my dad try to free *Ivy* from prison–

I didn't realize that I had dropped my acorn until I heard an exclamation of pain from below me. I leaned forward, balancing myself on an unstable branch and preparing to apologize–

"Jessi?" Ethan asked, staring up at me, his eyebrows raised. "What are you doing all alone in a *tree*?"

"Um, nothing," I responded quickly. "Sorry about that. I'll come down–"

"No, actually," Ethan interrupted, looking the tree up

and down before advancing toward it. "I'll come up."

"Oh. Okay," I said, caught off-guard. Ethan didn't strike me as the tree-climbing type, but I wasn't going to stop him. It would be nice to not have been the only person who liked to climb trees – excluding Ivy.

Stumbling through the process, Ethan managed to get a good foothold and struggled up onto one of the lower branches. It was obvious that he had never climbed a tree before with the way his limbs were awkwardly placed. So, I offered him a hand and helped him up to my branch.

"Huh. Pretty relaxing view," Ethan commented, and I nodded in agreement. "So, back to my original question. What are you doing here?"

I looked away and shrugged, fidgeting with my ukulele charm.

"*Okay*, then..." Ethan trailed off, obviously not convinced. When his eyes fell upon the charm that I was playing with, a small smile appeared on his face. "Hey, isn't that the charm that..." He swallowed hard as if the words that he was going to say would take extra effort. "That *Anna* gave you?"

I nodded, toying with the tiny instrument. "It's my favorite."

Ethan was quiet for a minute. He stared into the distance, his brown eyes dull. I followed his stare, getting lost in the green leaves that surrounded me. "So, how's your memoir coming along?" he then asked, turning his eyes back toward me.

Damn, the Landers and their better-than-average memories.

"Fine, I guess? Drake was useless, and all everyone seemed to know about Annabeth were her sports accomplishments, and–"

"Jessi!" Ethan suddenly shouted, grabbing my arm.

"What?" I cried, shaking myself out of the daze that I hadn't realized I'd slipped into. "What did I say?"

"You almost fell out of the tree!"

"Did *not*!" I protested, but I noticed that my legs *were* dangling dangerously close to the edge of the branch.

Did I just almost fall asleep in a tree? I scolded myself.

"Are you *trying* to give me a heart attack?" Ethan remarked in a frustrated tone. "Are..." He trailed off, studying my face and frowning. "Are you okay?"

"I'm fine," I replied, blinking hard to keep myself from dozing off again.

"You look... tired," Ethan stated after a pause that made him seem as if he was afraid of saying something wrong.

"What a nice way to put it." I laughed, but even that sounded as if I barely had any energy. "I know, I look like a disaster. Compared to last Tuesday, though, do I look worse or better? I think I was more pathetic then, but, hey–"

"Seriously, *are* you okay?"

"I said that I'm *fine,* Ethan," I bit back, a little harsher than I intended. I sighed and softened my tone. "I just have trouble sleeping sometimes. It's hard to turn thoughts off, you know?"

Ethan didn't look convinced but nodded anyway. "I

get it. My parents aren't the same anymore, and I don't know how to feel. My mom acted semi-normal around you last Tuesday, but she and my dad are so *distant.*" Ethan sighed. I noticed that he seemed tired too since dark circles were under his eyes as well. "Part of me wants to help, but part of me wants to just yell at them."

My dad is Ivy's lawyer. So, yelling at your parents is starting to sound pretty *tempting.*

Ethan twisted his grease-stained fingers in his lap. I knew that he must have been having a rough week since he liked to tinker with things – whether that was a homemade robot or a toaster – when he was stressed.

I chewed a nail as I waited for him to go on. From the look on his face, it was obvious that he had more to say. "Everything's so screwed up," Ethan continued eventually. "And Adley–" He suddenly stopped himself, looking away and blushing.

Adley? I thought, annoyed at the sound of her name. *What,* now?

"Adley?" I prompted, making sure that my face didn't look like I wanted to strangle someone. While I *did* want to strangle Adley, I decided that I would put up with Ethan's talking about her. It was the least that I could do for him.

"*No,*" Ethan responded, dragging out the single syllable. "I didn't say 'Adley.'"

"All right, fine," I mumbled, crossing my arms and looking away.

It only took thirty seconds of awkward silence before he tore a hand through his short, curly hair, then spoke again.

"I found Adley on my porch swing in tears Friday night." His face suddenly shifted into something that looked a little bit angry as he blinked and seemed to realize something. "Wait, aren't you guys fighting? Adley said that you guys weren't friends."

I hesitated. "It's a long story. I'm sure we'll get over it."

That *was the biggest lie of the century.*

"Right," he mumbled, looking down at his hands. "I guess Adley could have been exaggerating a bit."

"I'm sure that she was just upset and tired," I said through gritted teeth. It was so hard to keep my anger about Adley at bay. But I knew that the last thing that Ethan needed was for me to blow up at him.

Ethan licked his lips nervously. "Yeah, she *really* was. She almost–" He cut himself off again, his face turning pink. He exhaled shakily and closed his eyes. "Adley was starting to ramble, talking about everything going on in her life. Then, she was talking about me and–" He took another deep breath before admitting, "I *kissed* her."

I was a little taken aback. Ethan – to me, at least – didn't seem like the type to just kiss someone.

But then again, *Adley* was a special case.

"I knew that it was wrong – she's with Nate and all, but..." Ethan discreetly wiped away a tear. "It was stupid. I know it was. I just wanted her to know... I wanted her to know how I *really* felt."

I opened my mouth to say something, but the words were stuck in the back of my throat.

I get it, I wanted to say. *I wanted to tell Anna the*

same thing.

"I'm sorry," Ethan mumbled, watching a half-dead leaf blow in the wind. "I'm rambling." He suddenly smirked slightly. "I'm starting to sound like you."

"How funny," I remarked sarcastically, shoving Ethan playfully. He then looked away at the orange sunset, and I followed his gaze, admiring the view from our high-up perch in the tree.

What I loved about sitting up in trees was that you could get away from everyone. You could separate yourself from society's labels — because, in a small town, labels *defined* you.

On our branch, Ethan and I were able to escape the labels. He didn't have to be the dead girl's twin brother, and I didn't have to be the girl who was hopelessly lost without her.

Chapter 17
Adley
Gossip is Secrets in the Wrong Hands

The lunch bell had just rung, and students were racing out of the senior history classroom as I shoved myself through the doorway. By the time I got inside, only Jessi and Ethan, along with Mr. Fisher, were in the classroom. Faint R&B music, playing from the teacher's computer, was all that I could hear.

"Adley!" remarked the tall man from the front of the classroom as he picked up the pencils and papers that were scattered on his desk. "I see that Ellie delivered the message to you that I was hoping you could pass by before lunch. I'm happy that you decided to come."

"What's the problem?" I asked as I walked to his desk with my books in hand.

"Your grades in my class are the problem." Mr. Fisher shook his head disappointingly, then looked out the window before focusing on me again. I swore that I heard a snicker from the back of the classroom coming from Jessi.

"You're not even in my AP class, yet you're on the verge of *failing*. Now, I know that you may not be a fan of this idea, but I think that we should have one of my AP students tutor you."

"You *are* right. I am *not* a fan of this idea," I remarked, knowing that my statement must have sounded rude. But I couldn't help but be honest.

"We'd start slow and try to make it only for the next test," Mr. Fisher elaborated as if he wasn't taking no for an answer. "Adley, I wouldn't be offering this if I didn't think that it could help you."

I looked toward the beige-tiled floor, then back at him. "*Okay*, I'll try," I sighed, giving in. "So, who's going to tutor me?"

"Well, I was thinking that Jessi could," Mr. Fisher exclaimed. The wide smile on his face expressed how he was immensely proud of himself for the *worst* idea in the history of bad ideas. "You two were friends when you were both in my history class in ninth grade."

I turned my head around to look at Jessi. She stopped pretending to pick up her books on her desk and stormed over toward us. "Mr. Fisher, I really don't think that this   could *ever* work out," Jessi complained, surprisingly sharing my opinion.

"Oh," Mr. Fisher gasped, taken aback. "Well, I don't know who else could help Adley on such short notice."

"I-I mean, *I* could help Adley," I heard Ethan say from the back of the classroom, bringing a huge smile to my face.

"Mr. Landers, how generous of you," laughed the teacher, smiling once more. "Yeah, sure, if you're up for the task, you can definitely help her out." Mr. Fisher then walked to the door before adding, "Now, since this is sorted out, I've got some business to take care of. Feel free to hang out here for lunch."

"Thanks for volunteering," I told Ethan, turning to look at him as Mr. Fisher disappeared down the hallway. "But you *really* don't have to."

"And let you fail? Now, what kind of friend would I be?" he asked with a sly smile on his face. "I'm getting you to study, and I'll make you better than ever before."

My cheeks went hot, and I laughed. "All right, I'll be holding you to that."

"Anyway, I'm gonna go," Ethan said after a moment of silence. "I'll see you around." He glanced from me to Jessi, then exited the room. I watched him leave, smiling just at the sight of him—

Jessi tapped my shoulder, and I spun around to see her holding her books with a smirk on her face. "Wow, what a *hero*," she mocked, rolling her eyes. "I see you two have gotten close."

"You're acting as if we never used to talk," I retorted, not that her statement was wrong. The other night had changed us.

"Well, you never *were* the closest. 'He is just Anna's brother' were your words only a month ago. And now, *look* at you two."

"Ethan just wanted to help because, *obviously*, you didn't."

"Well,   thank God for   him," Jessi declared sarcastically. "Ethan Landers: the only person who's willing to even *attempt* helping a train wreck like *you*." Jessi's words squeezed my heart as I tried to walk away from her. But she grabbed my shoulder and spun me around. "Hey, I *totally* ship it. But watch out, *A,* because one false move and the whole school will find out how *slutty* you are. And kissing two guys on the same night isn't the kind of drama that fades away easily."

My jaw dropped, horrified by how evil she had become. But then, I decided to act nonchalantly so that I wouldn't look suspicious.

Who would've told her about *that night,* anyway?

"So, the shit you hear about me may be true. But then again, it may be as fake as the bitch who told you," I remarked smoothly as I headed toward the classroom door again.

"Now, does that quote you found in your Pinterest home feed make sense if that bitch was *Ethan*?"

Ethan?

Before I could turn around and grab her by the throat, Jessi strutted out of the vacant room and into the noisy hall.

I stormed out of the classroom, thoughts rushing through my head as if they were on a highway. I decided to let Jessi go and searched for the *real* betrayer.

I found Ethan standing at his locker, which was right next to mine. I slammed his locker door shut with full power to grab his attention. "How could you tell *her,* out of everyone in the whole fucking universe?"

Ethan's eyes widened in horror. "*What?*"

"You know *exactly* what I mean." I opened my

locker, shoved my books inside, then locked it so that I could focus on him. "How could you tell *Jessi* about *that night*?" I whispered as my face got hot, and the butterflies in my stomach squirmed anxiously.

"How do you know that I told her?" Ethan suddenly realized that it didn't matter *how* I even knew. "I *had* to talk to somebody, Adley. Like you didn't–"

"I had *nobody* to talk to even if had I wanted to!" I whisper-cried, tears stinging my eyes. "The only person that I would have talked to was *Anna*." It got quiet for a moment, and I licked my lips slowly before saying, "Jessi *threatened* me because she knows about *that night*."

"I only told her about how I had kissed you on the porch – nothing else," he insisted, trying to make the matter better. "As you said, 'whatever happens inside, stays inside–'"

"What happened to 'whatever happens *that night,* stays between us?' It was supposed to be a secret that we'd take to the grave."

"What if I don't want my feelings for you to stay a secret, huh?" Ethan looked toward the floor, wringing his fingers. "I like you, Adley. I always have. Hell, I may even lo–"

"Stop! Just *stop*, Ethan! We shouldn't have done it. We shouldn't have done *any* of it! I'm with Nate – I'm *always* going to be with Nate."

"And why? Why not you and me?" Ethan challenged. "Because I will always be your best friend's brother? Is that the *only* way you see me?"

"No," I mumbled, my heart aching from his words.

"*No,* it's not that at all. It's–"

"It's because you're not ready to break up with someone again, right? Because after Nate left for New York, you had told Anna that you didn't want to date anyone anymore. You didn't want to have to go through *another* breakup."

I was surprised that he knew about that, but I nodded. "Kinda, but I've also believed for so long that Nate was *the one.* I thought that I would be spending the rest of my life with him. I thought I loved him like that–"

"But isn't life meant to be *lived*?" Ethan asked me. From the look in his eyes, I could tell that he was serious. He grabbed my hand. "You're *seventeen,* Adley. You don't have to decide the rest of your life today."

"I just don't want to be alone!" Panic rose in my chest. I began to breathe heavily as the fact registered in my brain. "Because Anna is *dead,* and she was *all* I had. Because my mom is giving up on me, my brother's gone to college, Jessi is turning into a bitch, and Nate and Ivy were the *only* people left that I could turn to."

"You have *me*–"

"And look at what that did. I kissed *two* guys in *one* night." I sighed and quickly wiped a hand under my eyes. "Jessi told me that I should watch what I'm doing or the whole school will know that I *cheated* on Nate." I took a deep, shaky breath. "I can't let him find out. As much as I may want to be with you, Ethan, I can't bring myself to break up with Nate."

"So, you're saying that you'd rather be with *me,* but you're going to choose *Nate*?"

His words made me speechless as my head pounded from how overwhelming the situation was becoming. I didn't know what to say.

Ethan made an incredible point.

"I don't want to lose the only person that I can trust if things end badly. That's why I don't want to find out what *this* could be like – even *if* I want to. I know I shouldn't worry about the ending when it hasn't even started, but..." I trailed off, looking down at the ground. Then, I caught my eyes on my hand cupped in his. I pulled my hand out of his grip no matter how much I wanted to continue feeling his touch. After clearing my voice and wiping my eyes again, trying to look as if nothing had happened, I remarked, "Nate can just *never* find out, okay?"

"Find out about what?"

Turning around from looking at Ethan, I noticed Nate staring at us, his facial features twisted in worry. I stumbled backward in shock, squishing Ethan against the lockers as I felt his breath on my neck.

"Nate!" I cried, wiping the remaining tears from my eyes. "Now, why would we tell you if it's meant to be a *surprise*?"

"Yeah," Ethan added from behind me as I advanced toward Nate. "Who-who would want to ruin something *this big*? You should just walk away and pretend that you never heard any of this."

"We should be leaving for lunch, anyway," I told Nate, linking my arm with his. I felt super guilty doing so after the conversation with Ethan, but I had to keep up the act.

"Tell me," Nate demanded. He looked into my eyes,

and it was like he knew something was up.

I knew that I couldn't admit the truth in a *million years*, but I couldn't stay silent either.

"*Fine*, you caught us," I laughed as I looked at Ethan, who looked as if he was about to run away in a panic. "Since you're turning eighteen the week before Halloween, Ethan and I were planning a surprise party on Halloween night for you!"

A look of relief passed over Ethan, and he chuckled too. "I guess we're gonna have to rename the party. You know, now that it isn't a *surprise*." He was laying on the lie a little too thick. But I smiled at Nate, praying that it would slip under his radar.

"You guys!" Nate cried as he wrapped me in his arm and pulled Ethan over to join the hug. I caught Ethan's quick reaction of disgust. "You didn't have to go through *all* of this trouble for *me*."

"Of course, we did. You know how much I like you," I remarked as Ethan awkwardly removed himself from the hug, deciding to lean against his locker. I kissed Nate to continue playing the role of his girlfriend, though it didn't feel the same as kissing Ethan.

I actually found myself missing Ethan even though he was standing by my side.

"Okay, then. I never heard *anything*," Nate told us, winking a hazel eye. "I'll be totally surprised the night of the party – I'm an amazing actor, you know." As if forgetting that we were supposed to be going to lunch together, Nate then started walking away with a wide smile on his face.

Once he was completely out of earshot, Ethan turned

to glare at me. I could immediately see the rage bubbling inside of him. "A *party,* huh? Was that the *best* excuse you had?"

"It's been a while," Ivy remarked with a smirk, leaning back in her chair across the table from me.

A week after Ivy was arrested, I decided to visit her during visiting hours. We were now sitting at a small table in the contact visiting room. It was nice besides how Ivy was handcuffed to the table and a guard was lingering next to the door, watching our every move.

Ivy looked miserable – and I couldn't blame her. The police department had stuck her in a bright orange, button-up jumpsuit, and her green-streaked, black hair was full of tangles and pulled back into a loose ponytail.

"How are you doing?" I asked, even though the answer was obvious. I tried to not let the guard's stare creep me out too much.

"How do you *think* I am?" Ivy laughed bitterly, looking down at herself. "This place is Hell. I can't believe I'm even in here in the first place," she groaned, slightly leaning back in her wooden chair. "At least the good news is that if the first court hearing goes well on Friday, and I'm proven not guilty, I'll be able to get out of here."

"Wow, that's amazing," I exclaimed, trying to sound thrilled for my friend. But I was suddenly terrified for my sake – if she got out, it meant that I could have been a possible suspect again. "Your mom found a lawyer?"

Ivy's face twisted into a glare. "Yeah, it's actually Mr. Alvarez." My mouth fell open at the fact that Jessi's dad was helping Ivy, of all people. "Surprising, I know," Ivy laughed humorlessly, "because even though the police had told me that the tips were all anonymous, I bet that every single one had come from *his* daughter. She *must* be framing me. After all, *she* knew every word of our conversation at GV *and* was standing there at the cemetery right before accusing me of the vandalism."

The mention of the night at the cemetery got me thinking. An important question came to mind. "*Did* you destroy Anna's grave, though?"

Ivy's eyes widened as if I was asking her if she had gone to the 50% off perfume sale at Bath & Body Works last weekend. "Of course, *not*! How could you even suspect me of that? It was probably Short Stack's screwed-up version of revenge."

If it had been a few weeks ago, I would have thought that Ivy was the insane one. But *now*, who *knew* what Jessi Alvarez could do?

"What *happened* between you two?" I blurted, not seeming to remember why Ivy and Jessi hated each other so much. They had barely spoken since I met Jessi.

"Beats me. Sure, I like to call her names – who *doesn't*? – but she had begun to take them *too* seriously. Eventually, she was ignoring me, and all I had become to her was that classic neighborhood bad girl."

"Yeah, she *always* acts as if *she's* the little saint..." I trailed off, looking away from Ivy and barely keeping my emotions in check. The guilt kept biting at me like a rabid animal.

"*Keep it together,*" I heard a voice say behind me.

"I'm trying," Ivy whispered, taking the words out of my mouth.

Wait, what? Who is she talking to?

I turned around to look behind me. I then saw Damion – his chocolate-brown hair slicked back, his leather jacket draped over his shoulders, and the overconfident smile on his face distracting me from his scary eyes.

I ignored his presence and looked back at Ivy, still confused. "Who-who did you just talk to?"

Ivy glanced up from staring at her feet. A reaction of sheer panic took over her as if I was her math teacher who had just found her sleeping during class. "I-I wasn't talking to anyone," Ivy stuttered. "I-I never said anything."

Still puzzled, I glanced around again. But no matter where I looked, I couldn't see anyone but Damion in the empty visiting room of the police station.

"Are you okay?" Ivy asked me, bringing my attention to her. I noticed that her expression had gone back to her usual bored-out-of-her-mind look. "Are you waiting for someone?"

I shook my head and stood up rapidly, pushing my chair backward. "No, but I've got to go. I hope that the hearing goes well, and I'm so sorry about everything."

"A, what have I told you before? Stop apologizing for things that you didn't do."

But I did do this, Ivy, I wanted to tell her. *I am the reason that you're here.*

And once they would release her, as much as I wanted her out of this dump, I was then going to be on the radar again. Plus, this time, I wouldn't have anyone else to blame Annabeth's murder on.

It would all soon lead to *me*.

Chapter 18
Jessi
Some People Just Want to Watch the World Burn

Parties? They had never been my thing – too loud, too fake, too forced – and there were way too many people for my liking.

But there I was, at the annual Ember Falls High First of October Bonfire.

Mixing teenagers with fire. Wonderful idea, isn't it?

While it definitely sounded like a bad joke, the bonfire was a tradition in Ember Falls, and there hadn't been any incidents – well, besides the one time that Dylan had caught his sweater on fire.

I stared at the bonfire from my perch on a nearby tree branch, watching the flickering glow from the red-orange flames as they cast shadows on the ground. The sky was fading from indigo to black, and the first stars were beginning to twinkle.

"You coming, Jess? You're not gonna spend all night

up there, are you?" I looked down to see Annabeth in a white T-shirt and a pair of blue denim shorts. She was standing on the grass with her hands on her hips as her blonde curls billowed in the evening breeze. "Well? Aren't you coming?" she asked, cocking her head to the side.

"Oh, um... I don't know," I responded, chewing a nail. "It's nice up here."

"Come on, Little J! Where's your adventurous spirit?"

"Up in this tree," I huffed, just loud enough for Anna to hear me.

I could practically hear Anna's eye roll. "You know, being social won't hurt you."

"Fine," I sighed, dragging out the single word as long as humanly possible. I hopped down from my tree branch, landing ungracefully next to Anna, who smiled triumphantly at me.

We walked for a few minutes, watching our step to make sure we didn't bump into any of the older kids, who may have been drunk and wanted to start up a fight. Once we got closer to the bonfire, I spotted Adley and Ethan — along with his three idiotic friends. Dylan was enthusiastically telling a story. But while Ethan, Calvin, and Kyle were listening, Adley clearly seemed to prefer to be thrown into the fire. That was what the constant rolling of her eyes and the look of boredom on her face displayed, at least. When Adley spotted Anna, however, her face lit up — both with joy and relief. She patted the spot next to her on the grass.

Anna sat down next to Adley, stretching out her long legs. I took a seat beside Anna, tucking my knees under my *chin. Adley then started gossiping with Anna about something – whether it was real or in a TV show, I had no idea. And Kyle was suddenly arguing with Dylan, while Calvin and Ethan watched, sharing an exasperated look.*

I, on the other hand, decided to watch the fire's sparks pop and drift into the cool breeze, which calmed me. I sometimes felt like the "odd one out" among my friends. After all, I rarely had stories to tell, I didn't have any boys to gush over, and I couldn't keep a conversation going for more than a minute.

Everyone had their roles, but I wasn't exactly sure where I fit.

Of course, I have a role, I reassured myself constantly. Anna cares about me, and that's what's important.

After gazing at the fire for a few minutes, a glint of gold from near Anna's foot suddenly caught my eye. I searched for its source, tilting my head from side to side to try to get the light to hit the gold perfectly. When I did spot the glint again, I realized that it wasn't near Anna's foot – it was on it.

In the dim evening light, I could make out a small circle and a pair of wings drawn in gold on Anna's ankle. It must have been drawn with the brand-new tattoo pens that Anna got for her birthday.

I peered more closely at it, then asked her, "Hey, what's that?"

Anna's smile faded as her eyes fell upon the tattoo that I was pointing at. She pulled her white crew sock higher, attempting to conceal the design. "Nothing. Just a random doodle."

"It's really nice–" I started, hoping that I hadn't offended her.

"It's nothing, *Jessi," Anna snapped. I bit my lip nervously – when Anna used my real name, it was* not *a good sign. She sighed, then stuck a smile on her face. "Your hair is just chronically messy, huh?" she randomly pointed out, ruffling my short bob of copper-streaked, deep brown hair.*

That was an abrupt subject change.

"Oh, um, yeah," I responded, feeling my cheeks burn.

"You know what you should do? I think a leave-in conditioner would help, and..."

I listened patiently as Anna went through the whole repertoire of oils and sprays that I should try. But something about her tone felt odd to me – it was too rushed and stressed. It was as if she was trying to cover up something.

That little angel tattoo...

"Jessi?"

"I'm paying attention!" I cried, even though I could barely remember anything that Anna had been listing. "I'll find some conditioner."

"What?"

I blinked, resurfacing from the flashback of ninth grade. I found Ethan staring up at me as I still sat in the tree. "Oh, hey, Ethan," I laughed, hopping down from my perch on the branch. I then accidentally spilled the cup of punch that I had snatched earlier on his brand-new-looking Vans and frowned. "Whoops, sorry."

"How *could* you?" Ethan shouted, his dark eyes

narrowing at me.

"Jeez, I *said* I was sorry."

"How could you do that? To me, to her, to *us*?"

I had a feeling that he wasn't talking about spilled punch anymore. "You're being freaking *vague*, Ethan."

"You *threatened* Adley with what *I* told you! You're actually willing to expose *our secret* just for your petty little feud?"

"Petty little feud" is putting it mildly.

"Adley's the one to blame here," I protested, ignoring Ethan's question. *"I'm* just playing the cards that I've been dealt — fighting fire with fire. Annabeth would be proud."

Ethan sighed, crossing his arms over his chest. "You always wanted to live up to Anna's image," he remarked as his cheeks flushed red. "I could see it in your eyes."

"True, but didn't Anna play dirty when necessary?"

Ethan's eyes blazed with an unfamiliar fury. *"You* tell *me*, Jessi."

"I *am* telling you," I sneered. "It's *exactly* what she would have done."

Ethan's fists clenched by his sides. "It's like you didn't know my sister at all. Maybe she was a little overconfident, but she had a damn conscience."

"Oh, *I* don't have a conscience now? What about your pathetic excuse for a girlfriend? You think *she* has one?" I could see the hurt in Ethan's eyes but suddenly couldn't bring myself to care.

"Adley's a better person than *you*. And so was Anna,"

Ethan snapped, and I could tell that he was extremely hurt. "In fact, Jessi, Annabeth would have been *ashamed* of you."

"What the hell did you just *say* to me?" I shouted, my voice blazing. I felt as if I had just been punched in the gut.

"Annabeth would have been *ashamed of you*," Ethan repeated before angrily wiping his hand under his eyes. "You've *changed* for the absolute worst, Jessi."

"Yeah? Well, I *had* to change. After all, someone has to have a spine around here."

"I thought you were different. I thought you were trustworthy–"

"Oh, I go and say *one* thing to Adley, and suddenly, *I* am the villain?"

"I thought you were *different*," Ethan repeated, oblivious to my voice. "But I was wrong. You're *not* different – you're the same as everyone else." Ethan laughed bitterly, which scared me since I had never seen him so mad. "No, actually, you're *worse*." Ethan's angry, brown eyes glimmered with tears before he spun around and started to walk away. "Goodbye, Jessi. I hope you're pleased with yourself."

Not knowing how to reply, I spat a string of Spanish curses at Ethan. Then, I whirled around to face the tree that I had been sitting in earlier and kicked its trunk.

Anna wouldn't be ashamed of me, I assured myself. *I'm doing everything* her *way.*

Ethan had said that it seemed like I didn't know Anna at all, but it seemed more like *he* didn't know her. Anna would have never backed down from a fight – never would have settled for being second-best.

And that was what I was doing – winning the fight between me and Adley.

For Annabeth.

For her, I wouldn't back down – wouldn't give up.

That was what *she* had taught me.

After everything, I didn't want to stay at the bonfire, where I could possibly run into Ethan or Adley – *or* the both of them together, maybe making out behind a tree.

And behind Nate's back, no less.

Walking around the perimeter of the school's small soccer field, I paused to rub my eyes. The adrenaline from my fight with Ethan was wearing off, but my unrelenting exhaustion was resurfacing.

My nightmares were still the same – predictable and repetitive, but not any less terrifying.

I had attempted to talk myself out of the nightmares.

I had tried to analyze them.

I had done everything imaginable to get them to stop.

But *nothing* worked.

"Aw, are you three losers *practicing*?"

I felt myself stiffen at the obnoxious, unfortunately-familiar voice coming from the other side of the dark field – *Nate.* I pulled the hood of my navy-blue sweater over my head, hoping that it would hide me in the darkness. Then, I snuck closer to where I saw Nate standing close to Dylan, Calvin, and Kyle.

"Yeah, we *are* practicing," Dylan snapped, combing a hand through his hair. He pushed up the sleeves of his black-

and-white plaid sweater, and Kyle and Calvin shrunk against the soccer net. "Because we *care* about doing good on the team."

Nate threw his head back, laughing as if Dylan had told him the funniest joke. "Man, you guys *are* funny. Don't worry, I won't tell anyone that the real reason you're practicing is since you have zero talent."

"Back off, Nate," Calvin hissed, but I could hear his voice tremble. "Just leave us alone."

"You guys are lame," Nate whined, though it was clear that he was putting on an act to mock the boys before running up to Dylan and stealing the ball from in between his feet. Nate then picked the soccer ball up, tossed it hand-to-hand, and suddenly made a move that looked as if he was going to hit Kyle with the ball. My hands balled into fists, while Nate laughed, and Kyle flinched.

"Screw you, Nate," Kyle muttered. Even in the dim light of the streetlamps, I could tell that his face was an angry red.

Nate cupped a hand over his ear. "What was that?"

Having enough of Nate's loathsome voice, I stepped out from where I was hiding in the shadows. "He said, 'screw you,'" I repeated. Everyone turned to look at me as I approached them. "Which I think is well-warranted."

Nate dropped the soccer ball that he was holding and squinted at me. "Oh, look. It's the little freak who used to tag along with Anna and Adley."

"Wow, I'm surprised that you remember. I didn't think your brain contained that much memory space," I sneered, advancing toward him. "Don't worry, though. I unfortunately still remember Adley's *fabulous* boyfriend." I then smirked at the next thought that came to mind. "But *where* is your girlfriend? You should keep an eye on her. You never know what she could be up to."

Nate looked taken aback. "What's *that* supposed to mean?"

I shrugged nonchalantly. "Who knows? It could mean *so* many things." I heard Dylan chuckle from behind me and felt myself smirk even wider.

Nate seemed to struggle to find his words. When he caught me snickering, his face flared red. He then stalked off, muttering "bitch" at me as he left. Once his silhouette disappeared, I turned with a smile and looked back at the group of boys, who were all staring at me with wide eyes of astonishment.

"Damn!" Dylan exclaimed, looking blown away. "I didn't know you had that in you."

I shrugged, flipping back my hood and shaking out my hair. "It was nothing."

"You single-handedly took on *Nate Tucker*!" Dylan shouted excitedly before looking over at Calvin and Kyle. "We definitely need her help."

"Help with what?" I asked, my eyebrows going up in curiosity.

"You hate Nate, right?" Kyle asked, stepping forward.

"It *wasn't* obvious?" I laughed, looking up at the boys, who all shared a smirk.

"What would you think about joining forces?" Dylan asked, grabbing my attention even more. "We've got this plan – we heard that Adley's gonna be throwing a birthday party for Nate, and we had this idea to–"

I waved my hand, silencing him. "No, thanks. Leave me out of your boy drama."

Dylan's smirk curved into a frown. "Aw, come on!"

I shook my head. "Listen, I hardly even *know* you guys. Sure, I rescued you from Nate, but we're not suddenly best friends."

I don't need friends – they only disappoint me.

"Fine," Dylan sighed dramatically. "But you'll be missing out."

"I think I'll live," I deadpanned, then turned on my heel and walked off, rolling my eyes at the guys' ridiculousness.

As I trekked away, however, I couldn't help but think back to my confrontation with Nate and smirk proudly.

I didn't back down from that one. I laughed to myself, feeling giddy. *God, Anna, wouldn't you be proud of me?*

Chapter 19
Adley
A Thin Line Between Good and Evil

And that happened in 1862?"

"Correct," Ethan exclaimed as he placed down his color-coded flashcards. He high-fived me from across the wooden picnic table.

I had decided to go along with the plan of studying for that stupid history test, and today was my and Ethan's third session. We had chosen to meet up at the local park every second day so that we were in public and couldn't be tempted to do anything *besides* studying.

I knew, deep down, that something like *that night* could *never* happen again.

The park was vacant – the only other sounds besides our voices were the tree branches rustling in the cool autumn breeze.

"I think you're set for the test," Ethan remarked, and a feeling of relief passed over me. For once, I felt confident in myself for more than just how I looked. I knew all the answers, and it was almost as if I was handed the answer sheet every time I was asked a question.

"You *really* think so?" I asked as Ethan picked up his notes and stuffed them into his navy-blue school bag.

"Definitely. I have never seen you answer questions so quickly. But it looks good on you. Being smart, I mean."

I couldn't help but blush. "Really?"

"Of course. You're no Albert Einstein, but you could easily make your way there eventually."

We chuckled, then both stared into the distance. I listened to the roar of the cars passing by on the town's main road to distract me from how close Ethan now was to me–

His cold hand grabbed mine, and my heart leaped in my chest. I didn't want to let go, but I had to so that it wouldn't turn into anything more.

"I'm sorry, I shouldn't have..." Ethan looked down at his hands, shaking his head.

"No, it's okay. I'm the one who got us stuck in this complicated situation. So, if anything, blame *me*."

"Don't say that! If you're going to blame anyone, blame *me*. *I* kissed you first."

"And *I* gave in!" I argued, meeting Ethan's chocolate-brown eyes. "*I* was the one who kissed you back and decided to forget about Nate. *I* was the one who already had a boyfriend."

"*I* was the one who implied that you should stay over," Ethan reminded me.

"And *I* was the one who gave in!" My throat felt dry from screaming at Ethan. I looked away from him as my eyes began to water, the mistakes only sinking in now.

I had fucked up *everything.*

"You know, it's sad how we're fighting over who to blame," Ethan remarked as his gaze fell on me.

I wanted to meet his eyes but knew that I couldn't since I was bound to kiss him if I did. "It's kinda cute," I laughed awkwardly, staring at my black boots. "It's like—" I cut off my thought as I glanced up and spotted Nate in an apple-red sweater, his sandy blond hair blowing in the breeze.

"Hey, A. You ready to leave for school?" he called as he walked through the park's entrance.

I hopped off my spot on the table and grabbed my purse. "Yeah, we were just finishing up."

"Why are you two going to school on a Sunday afternoon?" Ethan asked as he walked with me and Nate out of the park's perimeter and onto the sidewalk.

"Oh, *you* are the guy that's tutoring Adley," Nate exclaimed, seeming a bit surprised. "I thought it was going to be some other nerd."

"At least I'm not some dumbass jock who can't tell the difference between the American Civil War and the First World War," Ethan mumbled under his breath before I elbowed him to shut up.

Trying to make sure that Nate wouldn't have the time to fight about what Ethan had just whispered, I quickly changed the subject. "To answer your question, Ethan, Nate has football practice, and I have debate team tryouts, remember? I said that I would try putting my amazing argument skills toward something useful."

"Wait, don't you play soccer?" Ethan asked Nate.

"I play *both*," Nate explained nonchalantly. "I play soccer *and* football in the fall, then basketball in the spring. Oh, and I play hockey in the winter, and–"

"Nice to know," Ethan stated, cutting Nate off as he began to walk the opposite way. "Well, I better go. Good luck today, Adley."

"Thanks," I called out to Ethan, smiling more than I should have.

The empty school hallways always felt creepier than they should have been. I always had this lingering fear that at any second, Ghostface would pop out from behind a corner and chase me down the halls with a bloody knife, like in slasher films.

Thankfully, though, that didn't happen as I waltzed down the senior halls in search of the debate team classroom. Soon, I fell upon the tiny room, which had rows of desks and multiple bookshelves filled with novels the size of a Webster Dictionary. A few students were standing around, either glued to their phone screens or chatting amongst themselves.

"Hi," I remarked, trying to get everyone's attention as I slowly entered the room. "Is this the debate team?"

"Depends," started an unrecognizable boy who had so much attitude that it took me aback. He had curly black hair, piercing blue eyes, and he was dressed in a white polo and a pair of brown dress pants. "Who's asking?"

"Adley Morgenstern."

"*Adley Morgenstern*," a familiar voice echoed from the back of the room. When I spotted a girl turn around to face me after having talked with another student, I tried hard not to roll my eyes.

At first, I had thought it was Lucy Montgomery, my archrival from tenth-grade phys. ed. class. Or even Marissa Langford, who had hated my guts when we both fell for Nate Tucker in ninth grade – but he chose *me*.

Any of them would have been much better than the bitch who stood in front of me, batting her eyelashes obnoxiously.

Jessi Alvarez.

"I thought that there was only room for *one* new teammate. That was supposed to be *me*," I stated as I walked over to the group. "So, explain to me why *she* is here."

"I'm simply here because I'm allowed to be and needed a distraction from *you*," Jessi snapped before anyone else could speak.

"Well, I'm *also* here for the same reasons. So, why don't you just make this easier on all of us and *leave*?" I concluded, crossing my arms over my chest.

"*You* started this. Why should *I* have to be the one to leave?"

"Because you're the one who went *against* me–"

"Okay, okay," yelled Attitude Boy as he stepped in between me and Jessi, who were glaring at each other intensely. "If you *both* don't want to back down, why don't we just settle this with a duel?"

"To the *death*?" I questioned, already prepared to fight for my life. "Because I'll kick her ass."

"Not if I kick yours *first*," Jessi fumed with a smirk on her face.

"No, a *debate* duel," corrected Attitude Boy, rolling his eyes.

"*Fine.* But I'll still win," I bragged as I tossed a lock of hair over my shoulder.

It was time to nail this bitch once and for all.

Jessi and I stood side-by-side, each leaning against a podium at the front of the classroom. The rest of the team had taken their seats at the desks in front of us, and I could hear them making bets on who they thought would win.

"First thing's first, ladies," Attitude Boy began as he joined us with a silver coin in his palm. "We'll flip a quarter to see what side you'll be on. Heads will be affirmative, tails will be negative. Your statement will be, 'Evil and good are black and white.'"

"Can I toss the coin? I do it *pretty* well," Jessi boasted. Attitude Boy nodded as he handed her the coin. She then flicked the coin with two fingers and caught it after it flew in the air. Once she turned it over, she checked out the results.

"Ooh, you got *heads*," I congratulated Jessi sarcastically before she could say the results aloud.

"And you got *tails*. I think yours will be so easy to beat," she theorized as she passed the coin back to Attitude Boy.

"I'd like to see that happen," I remarked before Attitude Boy silenced the audience and told Jessi to begin.

Jessi cleared her throat and straightened her posture. "Of course, there is a defined line between good and evil. You can't possibly be both at once. For example, you can either tease somebody with nicknames or call them by their *actual* name."

"Excuse me, but I call you *creative* names. I have no *cruel* intentions," I butted in. "And I can most *certainly* be a bitch *and* a good person if I want to be."

"The opposition can't talk until it's *their* turn," reminded Attitude Boy, and I shut my mouth with a scowl on my face.

"To go along with my point," Jessi continued after smiling at me menacingly, "good and evil are total opposites, as philosophers say–"

"*Which* philosophers, exactly?"

"*Adley,*" Attitude Boy hissed under his breath, sounding as if he was already on his last straw.

"I know, *I know*. I *can't* talk."

"As I was saying," Jessi mentioned, ignoring my original question, "evil is pure malice and destruction, while good is *not.* You're either good or bad because, while people *can* change, some part of them will *always* lean toward good or evil."

"Now, we will let Adley speak," Attitude Boy announced once he got the okay from Jessi to move on to my turn.

"*Finally,*" I sighed, feeling as if I was able to breathe again. "*I* believe that there's no clear definition between good and evil. I think we're all *both* and that our actions can't define us. Everyone makes mistakes – it's how people react to their mistakes that matters. So, *what if* you screw up one time? Or two times? You then know what *not* to do in the future. Someone can't be called 'evil' just because of their errors. After all, no one is completely good or evil. Sometimes, an event can force you more to one side, but that doesn't mean that's who you are."

"Well, if you screw up enough times, it *will* define you. At some point, you're going to reach the limit," Jessi interrupted. "You can only say sorry so many times."

"Well, sometimes people *are* sorry, and they *do* mean it every time that they apologize," I barked, thinking back to the night of Anna's death – to what I had done to her.

Everyone made mistakes in their lives. But sometimes they didn't know the true stories behind those errors.

Sometimes, people *needed* a second chance.

"What I meant to say is that none of us are pure good *or* pure evil," I proceeded, trying to forget about the other thoughts buzzing in my head. "For example, Jessi, only a month ago were you Miss Goody-Two-Shoes. But after Anna died, you *changed*. You became this bitch who goes above and beyond to be right about *everything*!" Then, suddenly, it hit me. "You're starting to become just like–"

"Shut *up*, Adley!" Jessi thundered. "Like *I* am any worse than *you*! You're the one who teased others for no reason, who did illegal acts just to '*fit in*,' who pushed her true friends away to be with the 'in' crowd–"

"I never *had* 'true friends' besides Anna. I never *pushed* anyone aside! When will it go through that thick skull of yours?" Jessi waited in silence before I screamed, "You *never* were my friend, Jessi *Cecilia* Alvarez!" I admitted, and I caught Jessi flinch when I said her middle name. "You're a lonely screw-up who acts as if she's the *perfect little saint* since someone so innocent could do no wrong. *You* are living proof, though, that an angel can just be a devil in disguise."

"Of course, *you* would know – not that you ever *were* a saint. You were born to be the devil and never tried to hide it." Jessi crossed her arms over her chest. "God, no wonder you're a cheater who can't decide whose bedroom she wants to sleep in."

The whole room turned to stare at me, and I felt my face burn with embarrassment.

Shit. She did not *just say that.*

Tears threatened to spill from my eyes, but I didn't allow them to fall. I couldn't break down in front of everyone.

"*Fuck you,* Jessi!" I spat.

Leaving the room speechless, I turned around and walked out of the classroom, calm and composed until there was no one in sight and I was able to let go. I smacked the locker doors that weren't shut, and some even managed to close on their own from across the hall. Papers began to fly all around me in the air, though I couldn't feel any breeze.

Not giving a second thought to the weirdness of these occurrences, I dodged into the empty washroom and let the door swing back and forth behind me. I held onto the sink's black-specked white counter, leftover water droplets wetting my cold, dry hands. My head started to feel heavier every minute that I stared into the sink. I felt as if I was about to throw up. I then looked back up into the wide mirror covered in dried specks of soap.

Don't cry. Don't cry. Don't cry, I told myself. *Stay strong, Adley.*

But I *couldn't.* Tears dripped down my cheeks, smudged my makeup, and ran down the front of my dress. I looked back up into the mirror after gazing at the beige stone floor tiles, bits of cheap, brown paper towel decorating the floor.

My long, shiny, blonde hair was perfectly curled. I had peachy lips and rosy cheeks. I wore a lilac, spaghetti-strapped skater dress and simple, black high heels.

I can't be pure evil, can I?

"I think you need to see yourself for who you *really* are," Damion whispered in my ear, sneaking up behind me in physical form. He was also dressed formally like the rest of the debate club was – a gray buttoned-up shirt, a pair of black dress pants, and a matching-colored belt. However, he was still wearing his scruffy-looking, black leather boots.

"Which is *who*?" I croaked, even though I wasn't up to hearing what Damion had to say.

"You're a half-blooded *demon*, Adley. Even if you can't see it."

I turned around to face him, and tears began to run down my face again. "Leave me *alone*, Damion! I don't need your fucking remarks right now," I yelled, pushing him aside as I walked toward the door.

He blocked my path at rapid speed and turned me around so that I was then cornered by him and the cool, white wall next to the trashcan. "You're not going anywhere. You think you're crazy for seeing me, but you *aren't*. I'm a part of you, and you need to *listen* to me."

"I said let me *go,* Damion! Leave me the hell *alone*!" I shrieked like a banshee. This time, I was able to shove him up against the wall across from me – *without* using my hands. He almost smacked his head against the small window's metal ledge.

He wasn't mad – he actually looked quite relaxed and put-together for someone who had just been thrown around like a stuffed animal. But somehow, he was able to corner me once more before I could run.

"Aren't you just a *tad* curious as to why you're able to do this?"

"I'm imagining things. I *can't* be doing this!"

"Yes, you *are* doing it," Damion cried before staring directly into my eyes. "Adley, this is what I've been trying to tell you!" Damion was smiling as if he had just won the lottery. "Morgenstern? *Morningstar?* Don't they sound similar?" I nodded but still didn't understand its correlation to the topic. "Adley, I've hidden this from you for too long. You *must* know the truth!"

"*What* truth?" I had sworn that I said those words. But my mouth hadn't moved, and the door was so close to my face that the handle had almost smacked my chest.

As the door closed, I noticed that it was Jessi who had entered the washroom and was staring at us with an expression of shock and confusion on her face. I didn't know what to say, and I knew that neither did Damion because Jessi wasn't supposed to be able to hear anything, yet she *had.*

Chapter 20

Jessi

There's Always a Loophole

What truth?" I repeated as I stared at Adley in the messy school washroom.

I couldn't *actually* bring myself to care about whatever truth the strange man was ranting about, though, since all I could focus on was how *familiar* the stranger's voice was. It was the *exact* voice that had been haunting my dreams for weeks.

Panic crashing over me like a tsunami, I whirled around and pulled at the washroom door handle, desperate to get out. But the door didn't budge – I was trapped. "What the *hell* is this? What the *hell* is going on?" I pointed at the stranger. "And what are *you* doing in the *girls'* washroom?"

Adley stood rooted to the spot, trembling. Her lips moved silently as if she was struggling to form words.

"*Answer* me!" I raged, my voice shaking. "What the

hell is going *on*?"

Adley didn't respond. Her wide, bloodshot eyes stared back at me.

"So, it's *you*," the strange man surmised in awe, his dark eyes meeting mine—

It was as if someone had set off firecrackers in my ribcage. I doubled over, pressing a hand to my chest. "Ugh," I whimpered through clenched teeth. "What the hell…?"

"Oh, yeah," the stranger remarked in an annoyed tone. "I forgot that *this* was how you creatures reacted to demons."

"What are you *on*?" I shouted at the man, who was leaning against the counter. He was oddly dressed in black as if he was going to a funeral. "*Demons?* How *old* are you?"

The man sighed and took a step toward me. "Six-hundred and sixty-six years old. Your ignorance *is* astounding."

"Just stay *away* from me, *freak*!" I screamed, then started coughing.

Adley, over her initial shock, stepped forward. Her facial expression was a mixture of anger and confusion. "What the fuck is your *problem*, Jessi?" she snarled, and I wasn't sure if she was referring to my coughing fit, our disaster of a debate, or the fact that I had insulted some stranger.

"*You* are my problem, Adley!" I bit back between coughs.

"*What?*" Adley scoffed, her voice dripping with sarcasm. "Are you *allergic* to me—"

I lunged at Adley, prepared to start a real, physical

brawl–

I was thrown against the wall, and my head was knocked against the plaster so hard that I could feel the shock in my teeth. I slumped to the floor, disoriented. "Ow…" I muttered, my head pounding.

When my bleary vision cleared, I could see Adley standing above me. Her eyes were wide with shock until I met her stare. "*What?* Did you think that I was too weak to hurt you?" She glared at me. "Seriously? *You* are the one who's afraid of your damn *middle name*–"

"Would you two just shut *up*?" the stranger yelled from across the room.

"What, Damion? You *don't* want to watch me kill her after all this time? Out of all the terrible things that you tell me to do, you want me to stop and be nice to *her*?" Adley laughed bitterly as she stared down at me.

"Maybe we should just listen to what this lunatic has to say," I tried, concluding that I would rather listen to his creepy voice than get slammed against the wall again.

"Oh, come on, Little J. Weren't you having fun? Where did all your fight go–?"

I pounced at Adley, somehow managing to send the two of us toppling backward into the sinks. Adley's head knocked against the sharp corner of the counter, and she let out a cry of shock.

"Fuck," she groaned, lightly touching her temple. Her fingers came away red with blood. "What the *hell*, Jessi? You're a fucking psychopath!"

"Maybe I *am* a psychopath, but that's better than what *you* are! You're just a bitch who–"

"Really, now?" Adley spat, shakily standing up with a hand pressed against the side of her head. "I think I'd rather be a bitch than a hopelessly, lonely psychopath who *no one* could ever love."

Once more, I went to dive at Adley but stopped short as my breath caught in my throat.

A faulty washroom light flickered, then went out. With Adley and Damion cast in an eerie shadow, the scene in front of me became all too familiar. The paper towel dispenser on the wall behind Adley had the same, semi-circular shape of a headstone. And in the strange lighting, I could imagine Damion's hands melting into smoky darkness. Then, there was Adley, who had her blonde hair curled, and she was dressed in a lilac-colored dress, a trickle of blood dripping from the side of her head.

Every single element in this room correlated to something in my repetitive nightmares.

"Dreams are funny things, aren't they?" Damion stated, but I didn't see his mouth move. It was as if he could read my thoughts. *"They're more real than you think."*

I wanted to say something, but I couldn't seem to form any words.

"A little ironic that all you've got in front of you is the demon playing the part of the angel," Damion continued, still not moving his lips. *"But it proves a point."*

"What point?" I shouted, my voice shaking. "That life is ironic? Like I didn't know *that* already."

"What are you talking about?" Adley demanded, oblivious to what Damion was saying.

I didn't answer her, too focused on listening to Damion's eerily familiar voice. *"My point is that evil will* always *triumph over good."*

"Funny, didn't we all grow up learning the opposite?" I retorted, which made Adley raise an eyebrow in confusion.

"Okay, someone *please* tell me what's going on. How hard did you hit your head back there?" Adley asked me before looking over at Damion. "Why are you two staring at each other as if you can read each other's..." A look of realization passed over Adley as she trailed off. "Holy shit! You can hear him too?"

"Of course, I can. Who *wouldn't* be able to hear his obnoxious voice?"

"No. You can *hear* him when others *can't*." It came out as more of a statement than a question, which puzzled me. "Jessi, I was never insane! He was right, all this time..."

"Finally, someone has come to their senses," Damion cheered with a smirk.

"Hold on, *what* are you talking about?" I questioned Adley, feeling as if I was missing an important piece of the puzzle. "I can hear your annoying friend. But 'hear him when others can't?' I think you *are* going insane."

"I'm not – I *can't* be!" Adley cried as she paced around the washroom. "For as long as I can remember, I've been hearing this voice in my head, telling me to do these crazy things. And all this time, it was Damion. Of course, I didn't believe it at first, but now? Jessi, we're either *both* crazy or he's *right*! We're..."

"Creatures?" I laughed in disbelief.

"Specifically, supernaturals.

But yeah, close enough," Damion stated. "As I was saying before, Adley's a half-demon."

"And what does that make *me*?" I scoffed, looking down at myself. "An *angel*?"

"No, don't flatter yourself." Damion rolled his eyes. "*You* are one of the Fallen, which are *half*-angels. They are known to be guardian angels."

"So, let me get this straight," Adley began, ignoring what Damion had said to me. "You're telling me that I'm a *demon*? That's why I've been hearing voices and seeing things."

"*Half*-demon," Damion corrected. "I make you who you are – without me, you're just a human. That is, at least until you die–"

"And I'm a *guardian angel*. That's *it*?" I interrupted, still unconvinced but somehow feeling a little insulted.

"Wow, that *is* sad. You got stuck with the pathetic role of a *guardian* angel – that's not even a real angel. It was as if you couldn't even play *that* simple role correctly. You probably failed angel school," Adley laughed cruelly.

"Exactly," Damion exclaimed, and I raised an eyebrow in confusion. "Well, the *failing* part is accurate."

"Are you going to stop being cryptic and *explain*?" I shouted, losing my patience.

"*You* creatures are mistakes. The product of a failed angel – one that took a crippling blow – and a *human*," Damion revealed, appalled by the words that were coming out of his mouth. "This is why you're also known as the Fallen. You have a sole purpose: to protect an angel that has come to Earth. Considering that your charge is *dead*, though,

I can't say that you're doing an excellent job."

"W-What?" I stuttered, my mind racing.

"You were *Annabeth's* guardian." A look of realization crossed Adley's face as she took a deep breath.

"What does that make *you,* then?" I shouted, trying to find a loophole in the conversation. All I wanted was for Adley to admit that all of this was just a cruel joke.

Adley didn't answer my question, though. She stood frozen in fear as if she was petrified by a thought that had just crossed her mind.

Okay, I'm done *with all of this.*

"You know what? This is *crazy.* You're all *lying! You* are the screwed-up ones." I turned and ran for the door, expecting it to jam on me again. It opened when I pulled it, though, so I darted out of the washroom without looking back.

Supernaturals don't exist – I'm not a guardian angel.

Because, if I was...

I had *failed* Annabeth.

I *couldn't* have failed her, though.

Once I was far enough from the school, I slowed my pace to a walk. It was a lovely day out – a soft chill was in the air, the perfect blue sky was dotted with puffy clouds, and richly-colored leaves rustled in the wind.

It's the exact kind of day that Annabeth would've loved.

Half-dazed, I glanced at the display window of Terry's Television Shop as I walked down Main Street, catching a snippet of the daily news–

I froze in place, my hands rigid at my sides.

Right there, on the Channel 8 news, was Ivy, strutting out of the police station. She looked a little rumpled and very tired but not defeated. My father was walking beside her, smiling proudly as Ivy's mother cheered from the small crowd that had gathered. The camera homed in on Ivy as she waved to her adoring fans, her trademark smirk displayed for all to see. Her poison-green eyes then flicked to the camera, and it was as if she was right in front of me, *gloating*.

If someone was listening closely enough, they would've heard the last piece of myself – of my sanity – crack, shatter, and fall onto the dirty sidewalk amongst the discarded gum wrappers and cigarette butts.

Chapter 21
Adley
In the Tall Cornstalks

Somehow, I had let myself be convinced – by *Jessi*, of all people – to participate in a get-together at the local apple orchard. This event was something that Anna, Jessi, Ethan, and I used to do annually on the Saturday before Halloween. We would pick pumpkins to carve and apples to make into pies after competing to see who could get through the wacky corn maze filled with puzzles first.

Though I used to always look forward to the corn maze, that year, I was not feeling it.

Jessi, though, had been obnoxiously insisting for months that we do it "for Anna." Oddly, I had found myself giving in to Jessi's requests on one condition: that Ivy and Nate joined us.

After the incident in the washroom the week before, I had thought that Jessi would abandon the plans – but apparently not. Instead, she had only wanted to do it for Anna even more.

So, there I was, standing at the entrance of the apple orchard and waiting for Ivy and Nate to show up.

I sighed, my mind racing with a million thoughts. I was still really confused, but after the encounter in the school's washroom the weekend before, so many things *finally* made sense. It now felt as if the last puzzle piece had been placed after getting lost for years under the sofa in the cluttered basement.

As much as Jessi didn't want to believe what Damion had claimed, I knew he was right about everything. Jessi was a failed *angel* – as funny as that was – and I was a *half-demon,* while Damion was my… sidekick? That part was still a bit unclear, though the part where Jessi and I were sworn enemies made total sense – we were always fighting about something. Jessi had also been so protective of Anna, and I was able to slam lockers shut with my *mind.* I was able to throw people up against the wall *just like that* if I was mad enough, and I would *literally* hear a demon whispering in my ear every day. My blood probably didn't even change colors when it was Tested since I wasn't fully human.

I was able to get away with murder.

I had *killed* Annabeth just because she was good – because I had somehow known that she couldn't stay on this earth.

Nothing good could.

The only fact that didn't make sense was how Anna and I were meant to *hate* each other. That was all bullshit – we'd had so much in common. How could *she* have been my opposite–?

I felt an arm wrap around my waist. I jumped, about

to scream until I noticed that it was only Nate, who had just arrived with Ivy.

"Whoa!" Nate shouted before laughing. "I didn't know I was so scary."

"I-I'm sorry," I apologized, somehow feeling uncomfortable in his grip. "You caught me off guard."

"Did we interrupt your nice daydream?" Ivy asked from my other side, her trademark smirk pasted on her face.

"No, I was just thinking."

Nate tucked a lock of hair behind my ear, then gasped. "Hey, what happened to you?"

I felt my face go hot as I realized that he had just exposed the tiny cut on my temple. "Oh, nothing," I replied, combing my fingers through my hair and pulling out the lock that had been concealing the wound. I didn't feel like explaining the fight in the washroom to anyone momentarily. "Anyway, we should go in," I exclaimed, changing the subject and stepping away from Nate.

Before Nate or Ivy could answer – or protest – I walked through the gate of the apple orchard, heading toward the corn maze. I froze when I noticed the group of people standing near Jessi in front of the corn maze entrance, though – Dylan, Kyle, and Calvin had found a way to join, along with *Ethan.* He often tagged along to this event, but I hadn't been expecting him to show up this year – not after everything.

"A, come on!" Nate shouted. I forced myself to continue walking, keeping a neutral expression on my face.

"I'm so glad that everyone could make it," Jessi exclaimed, smirking and crossing her arms over her chest as we approached the group. Her tone was so fake that, for a moment, I didn't even realize that it was hers.

Every day, it continued to shock me how bitter Jessi had become – how easily she could lie to someone's face as if she had grown up studying it. Especially since, just last year, *she* had felt guilty about how *I* had lied to my mother about my end-of-semester history test score. It hadn't even been Jessi's lie, yet she was the quiet and wary one around my mother for the whole winter break.

"All right! Now that we're all here, let's begin our annual cornfield race," Jessi exclaimed with a smile on her face. "Everyone knows how it works, right? We make groups, we have riddles to solve as we go through the maze, and the first group who makes it out wins."

"Wins *what*?" Ivy asked from the back of the group.

Jessi's eyes widened, glittering mischievously. "How about the winners don't have to pay for their corn maze entry tickets?"

"All right. I *guess* that could work," Ivy replied, and I could tell by the sound of her voice that even she was surprised by Jessi's new attitude.

"Okay," Jessi continued with a lot more enthusiasm in her voice. "For the groups, every year it was me and Ethan against Adley and Annabeth – and they were somehow *always* able to beat us." Jessi laughed as she looked out into the distance, surely recalling the memories from several years before. "But since this year we've got some recruits" –she said this as I watched her try extremely hard not to glare in disapproval at Nate and Ivy– "I thought that we should switch things up. Make it a little more interesting." All of us looked around at each other, seeing if anyone else understood what Jessi was trying to say. Jessi then pulled a plastic Ziploc bag out of her backpack and tugged the blue tab apart. "Everyone will pull out a slip of paper from this plastic bag, and the letter on it will determine if you are in Group A or Group B."

"Wow, it's like you *want* to be stuck with people you hate," Ivy commented, but Jessi ignored the statement.

As much as I hated the idea of possibly getting stuck with Jessi, it was a lifesaver. I *really* didn't want to become a tug-a-war rope between which team I should be on.

We all walked over and circled Jessi, then each took a turn to pull a slip of paper out of the bag in her hands. After backing out of the clump, we all checked our papers at the same time.

"I'm Group B," Jessi declared, "and I have dibs on being the team captain!"

"I'm Group B too," Kyle and Calvin said at the same time before joining Jessi next to the cornfield entrance.

"So am *I*," Ivy groaned as if saying the words aloud was painful. She then continued to stare at the slip in bewilderment as she joined her group.

"I'm Group A," I declared after watching the others react. A feeling of relief filled my chest since I was so happy not to be stuck with Jessi.

"Hey, we're in the same group! Isn't that great?" Nate whispered in my ear as he snuck up beside me.

"Um, yeah, that's *awesome*," I remarked, though my smile felt a little forced.

"So, I see we're Group A?" I heard Ethan say as he

walked toward me and Nate.

I felt like I was going to puke.

Shit, why am I stuck with the two people who have a crush on me?

"You know, you could always switch with someone on the other team," I implied, glancing over at Jessi, who was already instructing her group. "I'm sure Jessi would–"

"I'm Group A!" Dylan shouted, cutting off Ethan and running over to us. I noticed him cast a slightly wary look at Nate, but he quickly regained his huge smile. He nudged Ethan playfully with an elbow. "Now I can *finally* get to know the *famous* Adley."

"All right, people!" Dylan exclaimed once we entered the corn maze. "We have twenty puzzles to solve. So, we better move our asses."

Nate rolled his eyes. "We have to find the number signs that are located around the maze so that we can solve the riddles and get out of here, right?"

"Exactly," Dylan replied, and I noticed a harsh edge to his voice. "And I think we should split up to cover more ground."

"Are you some expert in this? I thought *Adley's* team always won–"

"Splitting up may not be the *best* idea," I remarked, cutting Nate off before he could start arguing with Dylan. "If I've learned anything from horror movies, it's that you should never split up – and the killer is usually a member of the friend ground." I felt my face go hot at the second fact, thinking back to the night of Anna's murder. I laughed to keep the moment light, but I knew that it sounded forced.

"Relax, this isn't a horror film," Dylan chuckled, combing a hand through his shoulder-length, brown hair. "Now, who wants to be with *me*?"

"I'll go with Adley!" Nate tried to cry out first, though so had Ethan. "No, *I* will," they yelled as my head fell into my hands.

"Fine, for *you two*" –Dylan gave me and Ethan a suggestive glance– "I'll suffer with Nate for a bit. We can then switch teams the next time we cross paths. How about that?"

After a few minutes of awkward silence, Ethan decided to speak as we made our way down a new path. "I see that you and Nate are still an item," he stated unexpectedly as if we'd been on his mind for a while. "When are you going to tell him about us? Unless, of course, that *isn't* happening."

I looked down at the dirt path, unable to meet Ethan's eyes. "What does 'us' even mean?" I took a deep breath and raised my head, glancing at Ethan. "The only thing that *we* ever do is kiss when nobody is looking. It isn't even a *relationship*–"

"But it *can* be. I know you are worried about being alone, but I know that Nate isn't the one you want. Either way, you'll be alone if you're with him or if you aren't. I can see you closing off from him." Ethan bit his bottom lip, thinking before saying, "He's like your safety school when picking colleges – you want him around *just in case*. But what happened to taking the risky road in *The Game of Life*?"

We turned a corner and walked into a circular area that was much wider than the recent path that we had been walking down. Four new trails sectioned off into different exit routes, and our first riddle was placed in the center of the area.

"Life isn't a game, Ethan. You can't just spin a colorful wheel to decide what to do." I wrapped my fingers around the ceramic plate that had the riddle written on it.

"Fine, let me rephrase myself: What happened to breaking the rules and being the *bad girl*? What happened to not having a safety net to depend on when things might not go your way?" Ethan stopped pacing and turned his body to face me. "Didn't you tell me once that playing things safe was cheating at life?"

I didn't comment. Instead, I continued to stare at the plate as if it would tell me what I was supposed to say next.

"Anyway, what's the riddle? Isn't this what we're here for?" Ethan asked after a moment of silence.

"It reads that the answer will point us in the right direction. What does that even *mean*?"

"Maybe we're supposed to guess the direction that the symbols below are telling us?" Ethan suggested, inspecting the plate too.

I squinted at the symbols, trying to see if I could decode them.

4 t n 0 5

Ethan stared down at it intensely until he looked back up at me and smiled. "These pictographs have to be a direction, right? Well, I don't think that the symbols are pointing anywhere specifically—"

"But the direction may be in the *letters*! Like, they must be spelling it out," I cried, cutting Ethan off as the idea came to mind. I blushed when I realized that I had stolen his words.

"Okay, let's see. It can't be 'west' since there are too many letters, and that crosses 'east' out as well. So, what about 'north'? Maybe if we shift the symbols around–"

"Or what if we read them *upside-down*?" I shouted, feeling the happiest I had been all day. Nothing made me happier than solving a tough riddle. "Because then, if you look closely, it's almost as if it says–"

"'South!'" we cried in sync.

I looked down and noticed a small image of a compass on the plate. I then realized that the arrow for 'south' was pointing toward the third path. "Let's go down there. It'll lead us to another riddle," I told Ethan before grabbing the sleeve of his black-and-white flannel jacket. After sprinting down the corn maze path, which brought us to another opening and a new riddle, I paused and hugged Ethan. "Life is too short to wake up in the morning with regrets."

"What's that supposed to mean?"

"That not taking a chance – not trying to make *us* happen – would be my biggest regret. I would *not* be able to live with myself if I threw away our only chance to be together just for a stupid *safety net*." I kept my arms wrapped around his waist and stared into his gorgeous, chocolate-brown eyes. It was as if he was putting me under a spell of honesty.

"I feel the same way," Ethan replied with a small

smile. "After all, who knows what'll happen tomorrow?"

I could tell that we had then both thought back to the night of Annabeth's murder, which only made me feel more confident about my decision. "I want to take the risky road, Ethan. I want to be with *you*."

At those words, which filled my eyes with tears, I kissed Ethan. I pushed him up against the next riddle's plate, which felt cool at the touch, and he kissed me back. I could barely feel time pass as I got lost in the moment.

This was what love was supposed to feel like.

This was what living was supposed to feel like.

And now that I'd had a taste of taking the risky road, I wasn't sure if I would ever be able to go back to playing it safe.

Chapter 22
Jessi
A Maze of Lies

While life had certainly stopped making sense a long time ago, this was a new level of insanity.

For starters, I – no matter how hard I tried – could *not* stop thinking about what had happened the weekend before. My conscious mind said that all of it was a stupid prank. But something inside of me kept screaming that everything Damion had said was true – and that he played a role in my life, whether I liked it or not. That was harder to deny than it should have been, but Damion seemed to be everywhere now. *He* was the shadowy figure in my nightmares that I still couldn't shake.

Thinking back on it, I couldn't help but laugh out loud about how messed up everything had become.

"*Finally* losing your marbles, Short Stack?"

I looked up from the pebble I was kicking around and found Ivy's green eyes staring down at me, her trademark smirk glued to her face. I glared and spat a curse at her in

Spanish.

"Yep, *definitely* losing it," Ivy laughed obnoxiously.

"And *you* would know because you *obviously* lost your marbles a long time ago."

"*Aw*, you're so *cute* when you try to be tough, Short Stack," Ivy laughed, leaning forward with her hands on her knees as if she was talking to a toddler.

Part of me wanted to yell, "Think *this* is cute?" and punch Ivy in the face. But I – with a supernatural amount of strength – managed to refrain from doing so. I didn't need to start any more problems with Ivy.

After all, I was sure that now that she was out of jail, Ivy was plotting *my* murder. I knew that she must blame me for getting her thrown in jail. And while she *was* partially correct, I hadn't been the one to find that final bit of evidence – her fingerprints on Anna's dress. But I knew that she would blame me anyway.

"So," came Kyle's voice from behind me. "Are we gonna start this thing or what? I only brought ten dollars with me, and I don't want to spend it all paying for *Nate's* ticket."

"Well, I don't want to pay for your stupid little friends' tickets either," Ivy snapped, clearly offended.

Ignoring Ivy, I turned to Kyle and smiled. I let myself slip into the Happy-and-Nonchalant-Jessi role that I had created for the day's event. "Yeah, for sure."

"Okay, what should we do?" Calvin asked after peering down the two paths that we were standing in front of. We were still close to the entrance since the first *simple* riddle had taken us a decade to solve. Finally, we were getting to the real stuff. "Do you think we should split up? We'd probably get more done that way."

No! I screamed internally. *Then, I'll be stuck with* Ivy*!*

"Sounds good," Kyle agreed, looking relieved – probably because he and Calvin wouldn't have to deal with Ivy.

I held back a sigh. "We'll do that, then."

Calvin nodded before he and Kyle headed for the right path. They then walked at a surprisingly quick pace as if they wanted to get away from us as fast as possible.

Since the boys had taken the right path, I started down the left one, hearing Ivy's rose-printed Doc Martens crunch in the leaves behind me. I wished that she wouldn't follow me, but we had to be a team now.

By the time we found a riddle, every nerve ending in my body was in fight-or-flight mode – having Ivy follow behind me like some ridiculously tall shadow put me on edge. I looked at what was in front of us, trying to take my mind off Ivy. There was an array of brightly colored sticks. With a closer look, I noticed that they all had numbers on them. I then saw that, for us to move forward, we needed to open a lock that sealed a chest, which would probably tell us which path to take next.

"Oh, look. I solved the riddle," Ivy suddenly declared.

"What?" I asked in disbelief. "How is that even possible? You need to know how to do *math* to solve this."

"No, Short Stack. You need to know how to use *pliers* to solve this." Ivy pulled out a small pair of pliers from her coat pocket and marched over to the lock, preparing to cut it.

"No!" I shouted, ripping the pliers from Ivy's hands and flinging them over one of the cornstalk walls. "We're going to play this *fairly.*"

"Well, I guess we're stuck here *forever.*"

I rolled my eyes, then looked back at the colorful sticks, trying to solve the riddle. I glanced up at Ivy a few minutes later, and all she was doing was lurking behind me. "So, are you going to *help* me or just stand there like a useless lump?"

Ivy laughed darkly. "You think we're here to solve some stupid riddle, Short Stack?"

I narrowed my eyes at her. "Where have you *been* for the past hour? The whole point of this is to solve–"

Ivy shoved me backward. I tripped over a rock, which sent me toppling onto the ground.

"What? Are you mad at me for throwing your *precious* pliers away?" I snapped as I tried to stand back up but failed.

"Wow, you *are* clueless," Ivy bit back, hands on her hips. "Did you forget that I had to sit in jail for over a week because of your little schemes?"

I scurried back on my elbows as hard strands of hay poked my warm brown skin. "You think *I* did that? Well, *I* wasn't the one who put your filthy fingerprints all over Anna's dress." Ivy's face flushed an angry crimson, but she didn't add anything. "I don't know *how* you managed to drag *your* sorry ass out of jail, but–"

Ivy bent in front of me and pressed a finger to my

lips. Disgusted, I smacked her hand away, wiping my lips. Ivy then laughed, "Short Stack, I don't want to fight. I'm just warning you." She paused, a smirk pulling at her glossy lips. "Make *one* more move against me and *everyone* will know."

Know what?

My face must have twisted in confusion since Ivy added, "That's right, Short Stack. I'm a *lot* smarter than you think I am."

My heart started racing at the thought that she knew one of my secrets. Which one could it have been?

"I can assure you that whatever you think you know is *probably* wrong," I snapped in an attempt to discourage Ivy, but I knew it was useless.

Ivy leaned forward with her face so close to mine that I could smell the cherry-scented fumes wafting from her lip gloss. "Oh, trust me. I know *plenty.* Like, I know that *hopeless little Jessi* had an *equally hopeless crush* on Ember Falls' golden girl." Ivy paused dramatically. *"Annabeth Landers."*

No.

I felt a blinding panic grip me as Ivy straightened back up, smiling victoriously. Ivy had always teased me, claiming that Anna had been my "little girlfriend." But I had thought that the teases had been *just* that – *teases.*

But apparently, they had been something *more.*

"I don't know what you're talking about," I mumbled, hoping that Ivy's idea would disappear from her mind. Better yet, I wished that *she* would disappear.

"Oh, *please,* Short Stack. With the way you used

to look at the Landers girl?" Ivy laughed cruelly. "It was *obvious.* I just never knew that you were such a *hopeless romantic.*"

My brain felt like it was short-fusing. I couldn't manage to muster any sort of reply.

Ivy smiled at me, flashing her pearly white teeth, and walked over to the locked chest. She suddenly snapped the rusted lock with her bare hands – which was apparently a lot more breakable than I had presumed – before bending over and reading something at the bottom of the chest. Once she was done, she disappeared down one of the paths and into the depths of the maze, leaving me alone and trembling in the dirt.

How the hell did she do *that?* I couldn't help but think as I stood up and wandered over to the chest.

I then peered inside to see that directions had been engraved at the bottom. The colored sticks must have been for the lock combination.

However, it didn't matter how Ivy had escaped. What mattered was that Ivy knew the one thing that I had tried so desperately to hide and bury from everyone.

Ivy knew the one thing that could *totally* destroy me.

Chapter 23
Adley
You Have to Pick One This Time

Oh, come on! You would look so good in this."

"Would I? I mean, I'm no saint, and white isn't my color–"

"It's like you're trying to fish for reasons as to why you shouldn't wear this costume, Anna!" I yelled at my best friend as she examined herself in my full-length mirror.

"I don't know, A. I think we should be cheerleaders again, for old time's sake," she insisted as she threw herself onto my messy, quilted bed.

"Didn't you say that since we're in ninth grade, we should switch things up? These costumes totally fit our personalities – I'm the evil one, and you're my better half," I laughed, which made Anna smile.

"That's what they think," she remarked with a smirk as she joined me in front of the mirror again. She held up the costume next to mine and inspected it once more.

"If it's because the dress is too short, that

wasn't my fault. My mother was the one who found these in the Target liquidation aisle yesterday. Besides, you're the one who always says that Halloween's the one time a year that we could dress up a little slutty and still get away with it–"

"Fine! I'll wear the damn costume!" Anna cried before heading toward the upstairs washroom to change.

When Anna returned, I was studying myself in the mirror and making sure that everything was on point – straight hair, short spaghetti-strapped mini dress, red high heels to match the dress, and the devil-horned headband that just couldn't seem to sit on my head right.

"You are so cute!" Anna squealed as she appeared behind me.

"And you look hot. I think we make a good duo," I exclaimed, looking at her through the mirror's reflection. Her costume was identical to mine, besides how her blonde locks were curled and she was dressed in white with a wobbly halo headband on her head.

Anna smiled wide, her blue eyes sparkling. "After tonight, everyone will know who we are."

"I've got to say, that costume *does* suit you," I heard a bitter voice say from the doorway of my bedroom.

I jump, startled as I snapped out of the flashback. I then looked back into the mirror that I was standing in front of and double-checked the witch costume that I had chosen to wear for Halloween this year – knee-length, flounce sleeve, black velvet dress; black beaded chocker; black high heels; lace-trimmed witch hat.

Remembering that someone was still present,

however, I spun around in their direction to notice that it was Jessi. To no surprise, she was dressed as Katniss Everdeen from *The Hunger Games.* She was wearing a black shirt, a pair of olive-green cargo pants, and a mud-brown field jacket, along with a pair of black topper boots and a quiver of fake arrows on her back. I was shocked by how put-together the costume was. But her copper-streaked, brown hair that was braided to the side destroyed *everything* since it was too short and stuck out like a pigtail.

"You know," Jessi continued, strolling into my room as if she owned it, "because you're a *bitch*."

I felt a rush of anger. "Like *your* costume is any better. It's *so* inaccurate since you can barely last in a Nerf gun battle."

"Well, at least I could last longer than you, who would probably *immediately* die in the Hunger Games since you've got *zero* logic."

"At least people could *trust* me. With the way you go around backstabbing everyone, you would never be able to ally with another team." I paused, laughing bitterly. "You know, you're gonna have to learn how to get what you want with more than just threats. It's a little childish, don't you think–?"

Jessi laughed loudly, cutting me off. "Aw, are you *mad* at me? Honestly, I think you should be *thanking* me."

"What the fuck would I be thanking *you* for?"

"Inviting Ethan to the corn maze, *duh*," Jessi said slowly as if she was talking to a child. "I'm sure you guys had *plenty* of fun, didn't you?"

I felt my face burn. I wanted to strangle the living

daylight out of Jessi, but I forced myself to keep calm, strutting out of my room. Unfortunately, though, I knew that my peace would be short-lived because I heard her follow behind me. She was laughing to herself like the psychopath she was.

I entered the ceiling-to-floor decorated living room, passing by the orange and black balloons that were stuck to the walls. I then walked under the streamers that were hanging from the ceiling and dangling over my head, pushing my way through the crowd that had formed in my house. It was as if I had walked into a 2000s teen flick — every teenager was holding a red plastic cup of beer, either swaying to the rock music blasting over the speakers or making out with their partner.

But how? I kept asking myself, freaking out every time more teenagers entered through the front door as if it was a never-ending clown car. *I definitely didn't invite all these people. Where are they* coming *from?*

I hadn't talked to my mom in weeks. I had spent a few nights on the Landers' couch until they told me to try talking with my mother, which I *never* did. I returned home a few days before the party, but I continued to avoid my mother every chance that I got. Luckily, I was able to have the house for Nate's party since my mom had taken off on a business trip yesterday and Caleb was staying in his college dorm room.

If my mom returned in two days to stained rugs and broken glass, though, I knew she'd *kill* me.

"Where is everybody *coming* from?" I shouted to nobody, straining my voice over the extremely loud song that was playing.

"Oh, they're just some friends of Nate," Ivy yelled casually as she danced her way to where I stood in front of the main entrance door. "But they *may* have brought friends as well."

I glared at her before rolling my eyes. "Who's funeral is it?" I then asked, looking her up and down. Ivy hadn't even dressed up, deciding to stick to her depressing-colored wardrobe. She was wearing a short, black V-neck dress and thigh-high boots, and black sunglasses were concealing her eyes.

Ivy removed the sunglasses, propping them up on top of her head. "I haven't decided yet." Her red lips pulled into an evil smirk before she laughed and added, "You know, witches don't even wear pointed hats – that would be like asking to get burned. Plus, they don't even look sexy."

I was taken aback by her statement. Especially when she smiled at me once more, then flounced off toward the living room. Her remark settling in, I removed the hat from my head and hooked it on the coat rack before finding my way into the kitchen, where Jessi was now standing. She was leaning against the kitchen island and scanning the room with disgust in her eyes. She was clearly judging everyone in sight.

On the table decorated with a black tablecloth covered in skulls sat multiple rows of unopened Pepsi and Sprite cans. There was also an untouched plastic bowl of scoopable Tostitos and a full jar of salsa. Of course, though, I could see through the sliding glass door that there was a keg sitting out on my patio. It was getting a lot more attention than anything I had prepared.

I was all for drinking, but I hated it when *I* could have been the one getting in trouble because of *others*. Plus, I knew that these rowdy teens would *definitely* be giving my neighbors multiple reasons to call the police in a few minutes.

"Nice party," Jessi told me sarcastically. She walked up to me and gestured around the house with her hands. "I have to say, I didn't expect all this from you."

"Thanks. Ethan and I planned it," I shouted over the music. "People will be talking about it for *weeks*."

"Yep, the party you threw with your boyfriend, for your *other* boyfriend," Jessi remarked as I tried to keep myself in check. "Speaking of your boyfriends, where are they?"

"Ethan must be here somewhere, and my *boyfriend* will be here any minute."

Jessi giggled sharply. "Still can't make a decision, huh?"

"I don't have any decisions to make."

"Just keep telling yourself that," Jessi replied with a smirk.

I wanted to snap back at her, but suddenly, Ivy interrupted. "Everyone, *hide*!" We all turned our stares toward the living room, where Ivy stood up on the leather couch. She was trying to grab everybody's attention by cupping her hands around her mouth to amplify her voice. "I just saw Nate walk up the driveway!"

Everyone ran around frantically as if it was the zombie apocalypse, hiding wherever they could.

I squeezed myself into the pantry closet, which was pitch-black once I closed the door. I only found out that I wasn't alone when I felt a hand slide down my arm, sending shivers up my back. "Shit," I whispered as my heart skipped a beat. "Who's there?"

"Adley, is that you?" I heard a familiar voice ask. "It's Ethan."

I sighed and found his lips, which I couldn't help but kiss slowly.

"I guess it's you, then," I heard him mumble as our lips parted.

The faint cheers of "surprise" and "happy birthday" then sounded from outside the closet. I knew that we should have walked out and welcomed Nate, but I couldn't. Pretending to be Nate's girlfriend was killing me.

"Should we go?" Ethan asked me, but I shook my head.

I then remembered that he couldn't see me. So, I said, "I can't. Jessi is bound to spill our secret eventually, and if she sees us *together*..."

I could hear him sigh quietly. "I know. I overheard you and Jessi talking before. I figured..." I could faintly hear him lick his lips. "You're gonna break up with him tonight, right?"

"Yeah, that's the plan. But I don't *really* want to wish him a 'happy birthday,' and then add, 'Sorry to break it to you, but we're over.' Sounds like a pretty sucky gift for his eighteenth birthday."

I was able to make Ethan laugh with that comment. "I know, but we could then finally go public," he stated before kissing me again.

I knew we had to go. But I kissed him back passionately, pressing my body against his–

The closet door swung open, and Ethan and I jumped back at the sight of Nathaniel Tucker. He was staring straight at us, dressed in his basketball jersey and wearing a red sweatband across his forehead.

My heart caught in my throat.

What the fuck am I supposed to do now?

"Happy birthday." I smiled widely at Nate as I stepped away from Ethan. "What do you think of the party? Pretty sweet, huh?"

"*What's* going on?" Nate cried in disbelief as Ethan and I stepped out of the closet. The music stopped playing, and everyone's eyes fell on us. "Adley, what did I just walk in on?"

"N-Nothing–" I stammered before cutting myself off, looking from Nate to Ethan. "Nate, I can explain."

"Yeah?" Nate raised an eyebrow. "What, did you *accidentally* kiss Ethan Landers?" Before I could try to speak, Nate shook his head, mumbling, "God, how stupid could I be?"

"*Nate–*"

"*Stop!*" he yelled, his face turning red. "How long has this been going on?"

"Just a couple of days," I admitted. I looked down at the ground, heat rushing to my cheeks. "I'm sorry–"

"No, you *aren't*, Adley. I can tell," Nate scoffed, rolling his eyes. "What sucks is that I actually thought you loved me. You know, I've always been there for you – I thought we were going to have a *future* together. Yet what angers me the most is that you decided to hook up with *him* – the freakshow, who I've hated for *years*." Nate looked down at the floor, probably embarrassed that someone like *me* would ever want to cheat on someone like *him*.

I was speechless and still trying to find a way to explain myself when Ethan surprisingly spoke. "What happened to when we were friends in ninth grade?" he questioned angrily. "More accurately, what happened to who you *were* in ninth grade? You were so kind. But now, you've stooped just as low as everyone else. I can see why my sister broke up with you."

"*What?*" I screamed as I heard the same words escape Jessi's mouth.

"You've got *another* sister?" Dylan asked, standing next to the kitchen island alongside Kyle, who was smirking. "Dude, how come we've never met her?"

"Wait... Annabeth n-never told you that-that they..." Ethan stammered, biting his bottom lip nervously.

"Because that was *history!*" Nate hissed as his face darkened with rage. "And *no one* was supposed to find out."

Then, there were screams.

Suddenly, Nate lifted his arm and aimed his fist right for Ethan's face–

It was as if she had moved at the speed of light from her original spot next to Calvin. Jessi now stood in the middle of the fight and had just flung out *her* fist, knocking Nate's arm away. "No one was supposed to find out, huh?" Jessi shouted at Nate. He kept looking from Jessi to his fist, surely shocked by how she had managed to deflect his punch. "Well, these are the kind of things that get found out. Hooking up with two people at once *never* works out — *Adley* can testify to that."

It was my turn to want to attack someone, but Ethan grabbed my wrists and held me back.

"But if you and your girlfriend — or, should I say, *ex*-girlfriend — want to fight about each other's *straying eyes*," Jessi continued, "take it out on each other. Beat each other up, for all I care. But leave everyone else *out of it.*"

"And what are you?" Nate scoffed at Jessi. "Ethan's *guardian angel*?"

Jessi flinched. But she pasted a glare back on her face quickly. "I'm just someone who can see you for the asshole that you *really* are."

The whole crowd let out a gasp. I could even see a smirk spread across Ivy's face from where she sat comfortably on the arm of the living room couch.

"And I think that *everyone* can agree," I added, having enough of the argument. "Therefore, I think it's time that you *leave*."

"Leave? Why would *I* have to leave? It's *my* party," Nate remarked. He looked around at the crowd in the room as if hoping that they could help him.

"Because it's *my* house. And I think you've overstayed your welcome."

"Jeez, chill. Now the party's over because *I* threw a punch?"

"Get out!" I cried, this time yelling even louder.

Angrily, I walked toward Nate. I prepared myself to

try and shove him out the door, but I knew that it would be difficult since he was a super tall athlete. To my surprise, though, I was able to push him extremely hard – as if by supernatural strength – sending him stumbling across the room. Everyone looked quite shocked by how easily I had been able to push Nate around. But somehow, Nate didn't seem as taken aback by my ability as he should have been. Continuing to channel my extra strength, I proceeded to shove Nate toward the front door. I had almost completed my mission–

A cold shower poured down on me. It was heavy – more than just a guest spilling a glass of beer over the railing – sticky, and gooey. It was as if someone had dumped a bucket of just-made Jell-O on me. It trickled down my arms and back like a waterfall of sludge as laughter echoes around the room.

Nate smirked in front of me. It looked as if he was trying hard not to laugh, though I could tell that *this* had made his night.

I turned to look at the entrance's full-length mirror. I then saw myself, standing in my once-gorgeous costume, soaked from head to toe. It looked as if I was *bleeding* – slime, the color of blood, dripped down my body and covered my trembling hands.

A flash of blood then blurred my vision as screams echoed in the back of my mind. I was suddenly taken back to the night of the murder. I couldn't remember much, but now, I could hear the spoons rattle above the kitchen sink. I could also see Anna's dead body on the floor, blood spewing around her head like a crown.

I could see the blood on *my* hands.

"Take that–!" I heard an evil-sounding shout from the upstairs railing, and I snapped back to reality. I glanced up and caught Dylan in mid-speech, who was standing next to Kyle and Calvin. They had probably snuck off during Jessi and Nate's confrontation.

It was when my eyes locked with Dylan's that his facial expression became more horrified than pleased. His eyes widened in fear, and he shut his mouth, biting his bottom lip.

Then, in his Dracula costume, Dylan dropped the bucket and sprinted down the steps. Kyle, in his magician costume, and Calvin, who looked as if he had tried to dress up as a pirate with an eye patch and some torn clothes, followed behind. Jessi emerged from the crowd at the same time to watch the show. Ethan also came out from the shadows, though his eyes were wide in alarm.

"Adley, that wasn't meant for you–"

"I don't want to hear it!" I yelled, cutting Kyle off. "I think you guys have just topped my night. I'm *done* with *everything.*" I looked back at Nate, who was now standing next to Ivy. "*Stay,* if that's what you want. All of you, do whatever the hell you want. I fucked up big time, but that doesn't mean that you have to act just as bad." Before they could say anything else, I shoved passed the gang and ran up the stairs.

Once I was at the top, I looked back to see if anyone had followed – Ethan in particular – but everyone stayed behind.

And maybe I deserved that.

I ruined everything.

And for that, maybe I *was* destined to be alone.

I felt calm and composed again – or the closest that I could be to it – after I showered. I had just finished re-straightening my hair and was now pulling out my old devil costume from the closet – it was the only other costume that I owned.

After slipping on the red dress, I reached for the horned headband on my dresser but hesitated. It felt all too real – it was as if wearing the costume meant accepting the role that I was meant to play.

Because Annabeth had been an *angel.*

Jessi was her *guardian angel.*

And I was the bloodthirsty *demon.*

"Wow, I have got to say, you truly wear that title well."

I turned around and came face-to-face with Damion, who was wearing his creepy smile. "Leave me alone, Damion. I need to clean up the messes that I made this evening." I shoved past him to get to the bedroom door.

As I opened it, though, I froze in place – *Can I get back out there and not feel like a total freak?*

Damion spoke again. "Bad night?"

Sighing, I closed the door, leaving a crack open to make sure that I could hear what was going on downstairs. I turned to see Damion now perched on my cluttered desk, smirking at me. He looked down at the books and papers scattered across my desk, then grabbed the first few books that he could see.

"What should we read? *The American*

Revolution twelfth grade history textbook?" My recent history test slipped from the pages of the book, and Damion picked it up. "Wow, a ninety-five percent on a *history* test? I didn't know that you could do so well–"

"Why do you have to be *such* a pain?" I cried, exhausted by his annoying behavior. "Can a girl have a break?"

"Now, if I listened to your wishes, what kind of demon would I be?" he answered, which left me without words as he continued to look through my items. Suddenly, he came upon a thick package of stapled papers and began to read the second page aloud. *"She acts weird around her friends when his name is brought up. She makes excuses to talk to him, even when she has nothing to say. She rejects him after he asks her to dance at the–"*

"Stop!" I yelled as I marched over to Damion. I ripped the booklet from his hands.

"I think this script is missing something – like a *murder*. And do you even know the proper layout for a movie script?"

"It's *not* a movie script. That part isn't anyway." I flopped down onto my bed and flipped to the script's cover page. "You were reading the idea plan for a script that I started writing."

"Sounds like the average life of an American teenager."

"It's   not!"   I exclaimed angrily before   he could produce more ways to insult my idea of creativity. "It won't be once I'm done, at least..."

"So, you write scripts?" Damion prompted.

"We all have our fair share of secrets, okay? Some people choose to cope with their feelings by writing in diaries. But I make scripts based on occurrences in my life. It gives me a sense of control over a scenario, you know?" I paused, shaking my head. "But it's stupid." I then caught sight of the trashcan next to my desk and tossed the script into it. "The person that I've become would never write about some secret crush on the boy next door. Don't demons have other shit to worry about, anyway?"

"Well, yes, but you've always been this way. Don't you get it? You have *always* been a demon–"

"Why didn't I ever do these horrible things, then?"

I slept with my dead best friend's brother.

I cheated on my boyfriend.

I killed Annabeth Landers.

Had I always been this bad of a person?

Chapter 24
Jessi
All the Games We Play

I wasn't one for parties, and this one certainly gave me more reasons to back up my hatred.

For starters, the number of people was enough to make me want to run out the door. *How* and *why* Adley had invited so many people was beyond me.

Then, there was the star of the show – *Nate Tucker*. He had always been a jerk – teasing everyone who wasn't a jock; cheating off other people's tests; shoving his way to the front of every line. But that evening, he had reached the limit. His finding out about Adley and Ethan was *long* overdue – and I *had* been anticipating the words that I knew he would fling at Adley – but his *attacking* Ethan?

I hadn't been expecting *that*.

When I had seen Nate's fist fly, something inside of me snapped. It had been a strange, sudden burst of anger and adrenaline – like I needed to *fight*. And oddly, that evening *wasn't* the first time that I had experienced that feeling. I couldn't remember much from the incident. But I *did* recall how I would have – had Anna not been there to restrain me – attacked Tyler Reed, one of her stupid ex-boyfriends, who she had been arguing with once in ninth grade.

There was the fact that Nate had tried to hurt Ethan – who, despite our continuing hatred, I couldn't watch get attacked. But also, Nate and Anna had been *involved* with each other. And, while I knew that Anna had dated *many* guys, that bothered me.

Out of everyone, *you picked Nate Tucker, Anna?*

I knew that I shouldn't be thinking ill of the dead, but I *seriously* couldn't help it. She could have been with *anyone*, yet she had chosen *him.*

Over *me.*

I leaned against the banister of the staircase, fingering one of my arrows. I scanned the living room, checking to see if Nate was still around. I was hoping that he had taken Adley's advice and hightailed his sorry ass out of the party. But if he hadn't, I wanted to track him because he was a perfect outlet for my anger.

I soon spotted Nate perched on a couch arm, smugly sipping from his red plastic cup. He looked far less distraught than someone should have been after being cheated on.

For once, I agree with Adley's petty anger fit, I thought as I glared at him. *Nate is massively screwed up.*

Looking away from the moron, I then glanced toward the kitchen and spotted Ethan and the three stooges. Not that I wanted to talk to Ethan, but I had a major question to ask the boys after they had dumped a bucket of slime on Adley's head just moments ago.

"What was that all about?" I yelled over the loud music that was playing from Ivy's speakers again. I walked over to the boys, then crossed my arms over my chest. "You know, I'm all for embarrassing Adley. But what did you *have* against her?"

Kyle stepped forward, placing his plastic cup on the kitchen island. "Like I told Adley, it wasn't for *her*."

"Who do you hate that much, then–?" I cut myself off mid-thought. I suddenly remembered the conversation that I'd had with the boys a few weeks ago on the school grounds. I sighed in comprehension. "Wait, the night of the bonfire, when you asked if I wanted to be a part of a plan... Was *this* your plan? You mentioned Nate's party–"

"*Yes!*" Dylan cried, exasperated. "If you would have let us finish our game plan, you would have known too. All we wanted to do was prank Mr. Perfect. Of course, Adley had to pass right in front of Nate and get the slime bucket."

"At least you got to prank Adley. *That* was a hilarious show–"

"Why do you hate her so much?" Calvin questioned, looking at me with concerned eyes. "Weren't you guys *best friends* a few months ago–?"

"We were *never* friends," I spat, cutting Calvin off. I then glanced over at Ethan, who was staring down at the ground in his Marty McFly costume from *Back to the Future* – his all-time favorite film. "You wouldn't get it."

"Guys." I was taken aback when Ethan looked away from the floor and spoke up. "Why don't you guys get some more drinks? I need to talk to her for a second."

The boys raised their eyebrows in confusion. But when Ethan didn't add anything, the boys shrugged and disappeared into the crowd.

I sighed, rolling my eyes. "Wow, you can't even say my name anymore. Am I that unrecognizable?" When Ethan didn't comment, I continued. "Look, if you're just going to say how Annabeth would be *ashamed* of me again, *save it.*"

"Jessi—"

"No, seriously. *You* should be ashamed of yourself. It was like you wanted to become a target tonight, making out in the pantry closet with Adley." I laughed bitterly. "That was a *majorly* idiotic move."

"It wouldn't even surprise me if *you* were the one who encouraged Nate to look in the pantry closet," Ethan hissed, and his words squeezed my heart.

"You know, I wish that it *had* been me!" I roared, a smug smile on my face. "But it had all been thanks to your loud kissing. I had just chosen *not* to stop him from checking out the ruckus. *You're welcome.* Now, you and your pathetic girlfriend can go public." I covered my mouth, smirking. "That fight kinda already ruined the reveal, though, didn't it?"

Even in the dim light, I could see Ethan flush bright red. "I had originally come to thank you for helping me out before. But now, I've just confirmed my theory."

"What *theory?*" I snapped with my hands on my hips.

"That you're a backstabbing *bitch.*"

I felt a jolt at Ethan's words — not because I hadn't had them thrown at me before. But because I could never have imagined *Ethan* stooping that low. "I see that you're learning from Adley," I said, laughing bitterly. "And you think that *I* have become someone different. Look in a mirror once in a while, Ethan." I then turned on my heel and stalked off, wanting to get as far away from Ethan as I could.

Part of me was starting to wish that I *had* let Nate beat Ethan up.

But Anna would've hated me for that.

After having a glass of Sprite to cool me down, I stormed off down the hall–

An elbow smacked into my side, and I winced in pain. I stumbled forward, just barely catching myself on the edge of a table. I glanced up and spotted the person who had barreled into me.

Green-streaked hair. Black clothes. Too tall for her own good.

"God, Ivy, would it *kill* you to watch where you're going?" I called to her as I stood up, though Ivy had already darted down the hall. Curious, I dropped my quiver of arrows on the floor so that they wouldn't rattle as I walked. Then, I cautiously snuck after Ivy, following her neon-green streaks.

Ivy ducked into a small, dark room filled with unloved toys and too-small clothes strewn about. I raised an eyebrow. She had entered some sort of storage room, I assumed, where Adley and her brother threw all their old things – but *why*? I pressed myself against the wall closest to the doorway and tuned out the distant sounds from the party.

"Ivy? That better be you," a voice called from inside

the storage room. It was a voice that I knew and not one that I liked.

"Nate, who *else* would it be?" I heard Ivy snort. "*No one* would venture into *this* dump."

"Hey," Nate defended. "It's the only spot in the house that no one will check."

"*So*," Ivy exclaimed, dragging the syllable out to change subjects. "I guess you and Adley are finished."

"We were finished a long time ago. I only stayed with her because you asked me to, remember?"

"Yeah. But seriously, you couldn't hold off on the breakup for *one* more hour?" Ivy sighed. "That was *all* we needed."

What the hell are they talking about?

"I didn't know that they were sneaking around together. What was I *supposed* to do – close the pantry door and pretend that I didn't see anything?" It was Nate's turn to sigh. "We'll find another way."

"No, *you* are going to find another way. I've done my part, but you fucked yours up."

"Come on, Ivy. Don't be like that."

"Be like what? All I ask is that you pull your weight for once."

"But I'm *so* much better at *other* things," Nate whined, his voice dripping with the same disgusting sweetness that I remembered him using on Adley.

"Aw, are you worried that we'll get caught?" Ivy laughed.

"Not at all. But no one can know what we're doing tonight," Nate hissed, all his voice's previous sweetness washed away. *"No one."*

"No one's gonna know. Adley won't even know what hit her."

"Literally or metaphorically?"

Those are probably the two longest words that Nate has ever used, I thought as I rolled my eyes.

"Both," Ivy answered, chuckling softly. "Because once we get her to the graveyard, it'll be *game over.*"

"Do you even have any idea how you're going to—"

"That's *all* taken care of, Natty," Ivy whispered. There was a pause, then the sound of fingers dragging across fabric. "You trust me, don't you?"

"Of course." Nate's voice had taken on an odd, husky quality.

What are *they talking about?* I wondered. *And why do they sound like they're—*

My thoughts were interrupted by obnoxiously loud sounds of *kissing* — from *that* storage room. Cautiously, I peeked into the dark, dusty room—

Inside, Ivy and Nate were in an intense lip-lock, Nate standing on his toes to reach Ivy. If I hadn't been so disgusted, I might have found it funny.

I ducked back into the shadows, my dark outfit blending in with my surroundings. I pulled out my phone to record them, then thought against it. That would take too long, and if they caught me, I would be as good as roadkill.

A photo it is, then.

Quickly, I peeked back into the room and snapped a photo before running off. I had used my flash, but it never was that bright. Plus, Ivy and Nate had seemed too caught up in making out to have noticed anything.

It was *perfect*. I wasn't planning on hurting anyone after the already-eventful night, but I *had* to take advantage of the situation.

I knew that I had to track down Adley to spill the news. Her seeing how fast Nate moved on from her would definitely take a toll on her – *and* it would make her hate Ivy too.

I flung myself up Adley's stairs, skipping a step in my haste, then darted toward the door of her bedroom. It was slightly closed, and I could see a strip of light casting onto the floor. Just as I went to push open her door, though, I heard a voice that made me freeze in my tracks – *Damion.* My first instinct was to run, but I forced myself to stay.

He's just crazy, I told myself. *He made up all the stuff he said in the washroom.*

I wasn't going to let myself be afraid of him or his words.

It's all made up.

But a small, annoying voice in the back of my head kept saying the opposite.

Ignoring the feeling in my chest that had sprung back to life at the sound of Damion's voice, I leaned close to Adley's door and listened.

"...Then, I got a huge bucket of slime dumped on me by Ethan's *friends*, while Nate enjoyed it all too much," I heard Adley complain.

"Oh, yeah. *Nate,*" I heard Damion's chilling voice tease. "That whole breakup of yours was remarkably interesting, by the way. You even managed to get that Fallen involved, which was *hilarious*. And, not to mention, you finally put your demonic powers to use when trying to kick Nate out."

"I-I don't know if I was *really* using them—"

"Don't try to deny it. You must have felt that supernatural strength." A creak sounded as if someone was pacing across the floor. "Good job on that too. Your demon side is truly outstanding when you let it shine."

God, he's still *going with the demon theory. Adley can't seriously be gullible enough to believe him.*

Adley sighed, long and drawn out. "Are you ever going to explain more about that? I'm kind of in the dark."

"I'll tell you more when you're ready," Damion answered.

"*When* will I be ready?" Adley shouted. "Because all I know so far about being a demon – sorry, *half-demon* – is that I can throw people against the wall if they piss me off enough. And that I can murder someone and get away with it."

What?

"It's a pretty nifty advantage, isn't it?" Damion asked. I could practically hear him smile.

"Not when the person I killed was my *best friend*."

No.

I stumbled backward, tripping over my own feet and crashing onto the floor.

Anna?

"Well, Annabeth *was* an angel," I heard Damion say. "She had to go."

"You made me kill my fucking *best friend*!" Adley

screamed. "All because she was an *angel*."

The walls felt like they were slowly caving in on me. But my body felt as if it was encased in cement and unable to move. My vision tilted, and I suddenly felt in danger of blacking out.

Adley killed *Annabeth?*

That *couldn't* be true.

Yet it made sense.

It was why Adley had run away from every form of investigation.

It was why she had been so happy when I had found reasons to accuse Ivy.

Because it shifted the blame away from *her.*

The *real* killer.

Adley killed Annabeth.

Anger suddenly boiled in my veins, replacing my fear.

I saw what this was, now – a *game.* And I was just one of Adley's pieces, being moved around where *she* liked and being told only what *she* wanted me to hear.

Adley killed Annabeth.

And she *wasn't* going to get away with it. Not only that, but she was going to *suffer.*

I would make sure of it.

Instead of calling the police right away, I decided that I would let Adley know that it was game over. I scrolled to Adley's contact on my phone and started typing her a message.

She would think that she would have time to flee, but she would be wrong.

She would have a five-minute head start, but that would be intentional.

She would know that I was on to her. Just that alone would *torture* her.

You don't have the upper hand, Adley. Not anymore.

Adley may have thought that this was her perfectly orchestrated game, but I was about to flip her game board upside-down.

Chapter 25
Adley
Better off Dead

No," Anna cried as she tried to rip the Nokia from my hands. She flailed her arms in the air toward my direction, where I sat on her vibrant pink beanbag chair. "They can't know that it's from us."

"That's why I didn't sign with our actual *names*," I responded innocently, afraid that she'd hurt me at any moment for making a horrible, newcomer move. "I thought putting our initials was clever."

Anna glared at me, trying hard not to roll her eyes. "Just give me the damn phone. I will take care of the message."

Feeling instant defeat, I threw the phone over to where she lay across her tidy queen-sized bed, her feet propped up on the stack of pink pillows at the head of the metal-framed bed. She started typing quickly onto the keyboard after I watched her fingers madly hit DELETE.

"We aren't going to sign at all," she declared

moments later with a mischievous glint in her eyes. "Our number is blocked for a reason." She rainbow-tossed the phone back to me. "I think this is perfect."

After properly grasping the phone, I looked down at the tiny screen.

Me

8:42 PM
Kristy, do everyone a favor and quit the damn lacrosse team already
Ur shitty throwing skills won't get u anywhere in life
Besides a mental hospital cuz u look like a total psycho
Every time u pass to a teammate

My smile was huge. "You are a fucking genius, Annabeth Landers. How you come up with these ideas, I have no clue." I enthusiastically hit SEND and got up from my spot to join my best friend. She was now standing up to change the radio channel that was playing on her digital alarm clock.

"Well, you aren't too bad yourself. I do take full credit for the idea of text-pranking, though." Anna looked back at me from her stare at the clock, shining that angel-like grin that could blind any demon. "Now, who should we message next?"

"What about Jessi Alvarez?" I thought aloud. Then, it was my turn to rapidly type a paragraph for the biggest loser in our grade.

Even though she was technically our friend, she deserved a message occasionally to remind her about how much of an odd bird she was.

"Um, okay. What would you write to her?" Anna asked, sounding a little less enthusiastic than she had been about messaging Kristen.

I had to think hard since I wanted to impress Anna. After lots of editing and rewriting, I finally created a flawless message. "How about, 'Spoiler alert! Cruella de Vil wants her missing Dalmatian back. Whatever you're hiding under that fur coat won't take forever to be revealed. Soon, the entire world will know how much of an outcast you really are. After all, we can all pretend to be someone we aren't — until we can't."

It was Anna's turn to be stunned. At first, she looked speechless, but then, she squealed. "You are a total badass!" she exclaimed as her eagerness returned. "This is definitely going to screw with Jessi's little mind. How did you know that she's hiding a secret?"

"Someone who acts as innocent as she does is always hiding something," I said, even though I had no idea what Jessi could be guilty of. "And it's bound to be found out about eventually, right?"

Everyone always told themselves that if no one else knew, they were safe.

But that never seemed to happen.

Someone was always bound to find out, no matter how deep people buried their secrets. It wasn't always about how that someone would react, or how much it could damage their lives. It was more about how that someone could use the knowledge.

After all, secrets made the sharpest weapons.

Jessi Alvarez had finally learned how to wield secrets properly, I noticed as I stared down at my iPhone and read the new message that I had received.

Jessi

9:52 PM

Spoiler alert! I know what you did, and you are going to pay.
You better run before the police get here because I've heard that prison isn't easy. After killing my best friend, though, you deserve to go to Hell.
You aren't who you say you are, I know that now.
You're not any better than a demon, related to one or not.
But after all, we can all pretend to be someone we aren't –
until we can't.

My phone fell from my hands as I staggered back, leaning against my desk for support. Damion picked up the phone and read the text message aloud to himself. Just hearing the words terrified me more than ever.

She knows.

She knows.

She knows.

The day after the night Annabeth and I had sent out those messages, Jessi marched up to us furiously during study hall. She had lashed out about how she knew that it was *me* who sent the anonymous text.

"Of course, it was *you*, Adley," she had snapped. "If you don't want it to be obvious, next time, don't call me a *Dalmatian*. It has come out of your mouth *way* too often."

She then told me that she was going to tell the *whole* school about the little prank.

She never did.

But now, I knew that she was serious about calling the police.

As much as my brain kept telling me that it would be better if I handed myself in than decided to risk my life running away, I knew that I *had* to leave town.

I started sprinting around my room, grabbing anything important that I could get my hands on – a duffel bag, toiletries, a few shirts, some pairs of jeans, a hoodie, my notebook, and my secret stash of cash under my bed. I shoved everything into the bag as fast as I could.

"What are you *doing*?" Damion asked in confusion.

"What do you *think*? I'm running for my life! If Jessi is telling the truth, the police could show up at any minute." My two bags were finally filled to the brim, so I zipped them closed and grabbed my phone from Damion's grip. "I'll leave this life behind and take a train. With the cash that I've saved up, I should be good for a while. Maybe I can get a job in the town next door. I'll restart and become a new person." I slammed my bedroom door shut and walked over to the window. I pushed it open as I breathed in the chilly October evening breeze.

"What about your family? What are you going to tell them?"

I didn't look back, though a tear slipped from my eye. "They'll soon learn about what I did and won't want me in their lives anymore. It's that simple.

Taking a deep breath, I hopped out of the window

and tumbled to the ground. The landing was softer than I had thought it would be since the green grass padded my fall. I stood up gracefully and looked up at Damion, who remained at the window's ledge.

"Are you *sure* about this?" he asked.

"I've never been more certain about anything," I shouted to him. "Since when are *you* the concerned one?"

Damion jumped out the window flawlessly and landed without losing his balance. "I'm not *concerned*. I just wanted to hear the words of certainty come from *you*."

We then sprinted down the sidewalk as fast as we could, taking multiple twists and turns down the back streets. The local train station was only ten minutes away. But I knew that before I got there and took the eleven o'clock train, I had to visit one of the last people in my life who still mattered.

I took a sharp left and ran into the town's cemetery – the worst place that you could be on Halloween night.

"Where are you going?" Damion called out to me, still following behind.

"I'm going to say bye to Anna." I stopped an aisle away from her grave, panting. Damion halted too, his eyes moving from me to the tombstone of my dead best friend. "It'll be quick, I promise."

"Oh, *fine!*" Damion waltzed over to a nearby bench, where he sat down to take a breath.

I kneeled on the dirt patch in front of Annabeth's grave and smiled. I noticed that the vandalized stone had finally been replaced with a new tombstone that looked identical to the original.

Now that I was there, I didn't know what to say. A tear slipped from my eye as I took a seat next to Anna's tombstone. I pretended that she was there, sitting next to me under the sheet of twinkling stars. After a few minutes of saying nothing, I decided to search through my duffel bag to look for my phone. I came across some pens, paper, a small bottle–

Freezing in place, I pulled out the see-through pill bottle, which contained only four red pills.

The ones from *that night.*

A sudden urge then took over me, and a compulsion drew me to the drug because I *just* needed *one.*

I knocked back the four pills before my hand and the bottle fell to my side. My body began to tremble. I knew that I shouldn't have, but even the memory of Ethan's words couldn't stop me.

I had a *problem.*

I angrily threw the bottle onto the ground and started digging through my duffel bag to continue looking for my phone. Instead, though, I came across a ball of paper. Only after unfolding it did I realize that it was the letter to Anna that I had written *that night.* It made me smile as much as I wanted to break down into sobs in Anna's arms.

I placed the letter down and hoped that she was reading it in spirit.

"This kind of clarifies everything, though I know it's not the best explanation," I began whispering. "I don't know *why* I killed you. I still need to figure that part out. As well as how I am a half-demon, you are an angel, and Jessi is your guardian angel. Did you know about this? Did you keep this from us?" I stopped myself, knowing that I didn't have much time left. "There's also the part where I slept with your brother, cheating on Nate. Sure, Nate had originally been 'Mr. Perfect.' But after your brother kissed me, I never felt the same way around Nate as I had that night with Ethan." More tears ran down my face, which dripped onto the dry. "I know that leaving Ember Falls isn't the *best* solution... If you were still here, you probably would have told me that I'm just running away from my problems. But now, all I have is..."

Ethan.

Just hearing the syllables of his name echo off the walls of my brain made me feel guilty for leaving him behind without saying anything.

"Shit, I need to message your brother. Hell, I think I *love* him, but I was too much of a coward to tell him. And now, I'm never going to be able to see him again." I wiped the tears away with a cold hand before finally finding my phone in my bag. "I love you, Anna. Don't *ever* forget that. I will find a way to get out of this mess and not leave your brother. I know that's what you would have wanted."

When I found Ethan in my contacts, I sighed in relief before writing.

Me
10:34 PM
As much as I don't want to leave,
I have no choice.
I did something rly bad, and

the police know.
They r on their
way to the house now.
I know that u may not forgive me but
I want u to know that I'm so sorry about
everything

A few seconds after sending the message, I then added, "I love you, and I hope you know that."

Surprisingly, only a minute later did Ethan respond. It was as if he was waiting for a message from someone.

Ethan
10:36 PM
Adley, I will always be on ur side,
no matter what u do.
Where r u? I will leave as fast as I can and meet u.
If u need to run, I will run away with u.
No matter what.

Me
10:36 PM
What? Ethan, u r crazy.
U can't leave ur whole life behind.

Ethan
10:37 PM
Yeah, I *am* crazy.
But I don't have anything left here,
not anymore.
U r all I have.

I paused for a second, trying to comprehend how this was *really* happening. Then, before reality could change my mind, I typed, "I'm at the cemetery saying goodbye to ur sister."

Ethan
10:38 PM
On my way.
And P.S. I love you too.

I never believed that four simple words could bring such joy and comfort. I smiled so big that even in the dark, someone would probably be able to see my grin. As bad as the situation was, the one thing that I wanted to hear, for once, made me feel the way it should have.

Ethan Landers loves me.

I stood up, brushed the dirt off my costume, and picked up my bag. I hated that I was a half-blooded demon, that my best friend was dead, and that everyone was soon going to find out the question that had been headlining articles and reports for weeks: *Who killed Annabeth Landers?*

But I knew that after everything, I would still have Ethan.

He was going to be my reason to live and survive.

He was going to meet up with me, we were going to run off into the light of dawn, and we were going to hop on a train that would take us away from Ember Falls. We were going to travel the world, just us two, and we were going to live our lives for Anna.

We were going to do everything *for Anna.*

I glanced at the screen of my phone, rereading the conversation that I'd had with Ethan. "This is what I want. This is what I *need*."

The wind howled like a vicious wolf, and I could hear the faint cry of police cars driving down a nearby street. I could see the flash of red and blue lights, looking like Fourth of July fireworks that couldn't make it up into the sky.

Then, I heard the creak of the metal cemetery gate and the rattle of bushes and trees swaying in the breeze. I could hear footsteps behind me, and for a second, I thought it was Ghostface sneaking up on me and preparing to smash my head into a gravestone.

But I knew that I wasn't in a horror movie – I wasn't afraid.

I knew who it was.

"Ethan?" I called, not turning around–

I felt something smash into the back of my head. A burning pain spread through my brain as if my skull had been crushed into millions of tiny pieces.

Black spots blurred my vision. My legs gave out.

I fell onto something hard. Panic rushed through me as a prickly sensation crept across my skin. It was as if a thousand needles were stabbing me.

It isn't Ethan! It isn't *Ethan!*

I wanted to stand up. I wanted to run–

I couldn't move.

I couldn't find the will or energy in my body–

I saw a flash of neon green as the last of my vision faded to black.

I can't die.

I can't die.

I can't die.

Not when Ethan and I are finally going to be free.

I had never wanted my life to end this way.

Not *then.* Not *there.* Not–

Acknowledgments

It's incredible to think that just a few years ago, I was dreading the moment that I would have to draft a short story for a class assignment. I never imagined that I'd eventually turn my creative imagination into something that so many people would be able to enjoy.

Firstly, to my readers – thank *you* for choosing this book and spending time with my characters. I couldn't be happier to share it with you.

Secondly, this story was so much fun to write, though it *did* take a lot of time away from being with the people I love most.

To Mom and Dad, thank you for always believing in me, for supporting my dreams, and for reading everything I write. Also, thank you for being understanding when I would lock myself in my bedroom and spend long hours writing and editing this novel to make it the best. I love you so much, and I am beyond thankful for you.

To all my family – especially my uncle, John, who was my first reader and a huge supporter – thank you for always cheering me on and being so excited to read my stories.

To all of my friends, new and old – you know who you

are – thank you for believing that I can do this. Your constant support – and crazy plot-twist ideas – have aided my book in too many ways to count. A special thanks to Alexandra Congonidis, who was a huge part of making this book happen – from creating story plots to helping me develop my characters. I can't even write into words how thankful I am for your inspiring and original ideas.

To all my high school teachers, especially Jennifer Goodall and Patricia Morrissette, thank you for reading my first drafts and giving me the constructive criticism that I needed. You have all helped me become a better writer.

To the people who have taken the time to read the horrible drafts of this story, thank you. You have given me feedback that has improved this novel *majorly*, and without you, my story wouldn't be the same.

This includes my amazing Wattpad readers and followers. I can't even put into words how much it has meant to me to have had you along for the journey and to read your thoughts about my drafts. I never thought I would get so many views and votes, and every read has meant so much to me. Thank you, from the bottom of my heart, for getting me here and being so supportive. I love you all to no extent.

This novel has changed me, and I can't wait to see what the future will hold for these magnificent characters. After all, you didn't think the story was over, did you?

About the Author

Enya Clancy is an author of dark dramas and murder mysteries, including *How to Get Away with Evil*. When she isn't writing, she could be found reading a good thriller or listening to music. She lives in Canada and enjoys binge-watching horror movies, writing poetry, and capturing moments through photography.